P9-AFY-878

FOR MEN ONLY

FOR MEN ONLY

SECRETS OF A
SUCCESSFUL IMAGE

Richard Derwald & Anthony Chiappone

Prometheus Books
59 John Glenn Drive
Amherst, New York 14228-2197

Published 1995 by Prometheus Books

The photograph appearing on page 18 is courtesy of Jeff Ellis. The photographs appearing on pages 30 and 150 are courtesy of Michael and Walter Mocellin and Barbizon Academy of Ontario, Canada. The photograph appearing on page 98 is courtesy of NordicTrack. The photograph appearing on page 160 is courtesy of Sharon Barber. The photograph appearing on page 177 © Frank M. Luterek. The photograph appearing on page 182 is courtesy of The Townsend Institute, Chapel Hill, North Carolina.

99 98 97 96 95   5 4 3 2 1

Library of Congress Cataloging-in-Publication Data

Derwald, Richard.
    For men only : secrets of a successful image / by Richard Derwald and Anthony Chiappone.
        p.   cm.
    Includes bibliographical references (p.   ).
    ISBN 0-87975-910-0
    1. Grooming for men. 2. Cosmetics for men. I. Chiappone, Anthony. II. Title.
RA777.8.D46   1995
646.7′044—dc20   94-24932
                                                        CIP

Printed in the United States of America on acid-free paper.

In Loving Memory
of
Katherine Ann Walsh Derwald
Margaret Rose Biasucci Chiappone
Karl Derwald

Contents

Preface

The intent of this work is to acquaint you with the various resources currently available to enhance your image. In our effort to provide this information we have named companies and individuals who we feel are among the leaders in their respective areas of male image enhancement. Discussion of these companies and individuals as well as their products and/or services should not be construed as an endorsement by the authors or the publisher.

Product photographs appear where indicated courtesy of the manufacturer or supplier. The authors emphasize that these photographs are for informational purposes only and do not constitute endorsement of the brand names shown. We wish to thank the following companies and individuals who helped make this book possible by contributing valuable information and illustrations:

Aesthetic Associates Center
2500 Kensington Avenue
Amherst, NY 14226
(716) 839–1700

Alpha-OMEGA HAIR AND
  SCALP CLINIC
8019 N. Himes Ave., Suite 311
Tampa, FL 33614
(813) 933–2136

14   For Men Only

American Society for
	Aesthetic Plastic Surgery, Inc.
3922 Atlantic Avenue
Long Beach, CA 90807
(708) 228-9274

American Society of Plastic and
	Reconstructive Surgeons
444 East Algonquin Road
Arlington Heights, IL 60005-4644
(708) 228-9900

Combe Incorporated
1101 Westchester Avenue
White Plains, NY 10604
(800) 431-2610 (Toll Free)

The Fashion Association
475 Park Avenue South
New York, NY 10016
(212) 683-5665

Hair Club For Men, Ltd.
185 Madison Ave.
New York, NY 10016
(800) 888-4236 (Toll Free)

Frank M. Luterek, Photographer
56 Capen Blvd.
Buffalo, NY 14214

Myosystems, Inc./MET-Rx
400 Corporate Drive, Suite J
Golden, CO 80401
(800) 637-1572 (Toll Free)

NordicTrack
104 Peavey Road
Chaska, MN 55318-2355
(800) 445-2606 (Toll Free)

Richlee Shoe Company
P.O. Box 3566
Frederick, MD 21705
(800) 343-3810 (Toll Free)
Maryland residents call (301) 663-5111

The Sinclair Institute
P.O. Box 8865
Chapel Hill, NC 27515
(800) 955-0888 (Toll Free)

The Townsend Institute
P.O. Box 8855
Chapel Hill, NC 27515
(800) 888-1900 (Toll Free)

Before We Start

If you are the type of man who would admit to being reasonably satisfied with his personal image and would say, if asked, that you have a healthy self-esteem, then we urge you to consider how you view yourself before and after reading each chapter of this book. In the pages that follow, we believe you will find some helpful tips, many useful suggestions, and valuable options for improving your image in ways you never thought possible.

Ultimately all questions about personal image must be asked and answered by each individual. *You* are the real judge of how *you* should look, not any book and certainly not society. When it comes to the importance of image, the only opinion that matters is *yours*. We have not written this book for impressionable men who feel compelled to buy into every new fad. Ours is a book for the thinking man. If you are truly comfortable and happy with the way you look, then you probably would not have picked up this book in the first place. Since you do feel there is room for improving how you present yourself to others, please read on.

This volume has been developed for men who feel the need to improve their image to its maximum potential. Many men believe that their personal, unaltered image isn't what it could be. They want to make selective changes because they sincerely believe that their professional and personal success depends on the way others react to their appearance.

Certainly there are men who, though not physically attractive, are both successful and happy. These men can be counted among the ranks of successful people in nearly every vocation one could name. And, to be sure, there are women who place little or no value on the way a man looks, but we think you'll agree that these represent exceptions rather than the rule.

We believe that people are affected by what they see and tend to make important judgments and decisions about others based, at least to some extent, on physical appearance. It stands to reason, then, that if you upgrade your image, it may well improve many aspects of your life by positively changing the ways others perceive and act toward you. Upgrading your image may not necessarily make you more successful in your efforts to achieve all of life's rewards, but improving your image should make you feel better about yourself, and there can be no doubt that a positive self-image is a prerequisite to success.

OUR PURPOSE

For good or ill, there are three things upon which the world judges a man. In order of importance, they are:

1. what he has,
2. what he does, and
3. how he looks.

The ultimate example of the importance of these three factors is President John F. Kennedy. Not only was he from a wealthy New England family and the holder of the highest elected office in the land, but he was viewed by the majority of people as possessing youthful good looks.

Of the three factors noted above, we will concentrate on the third factor, namely, *physical image*. It is our view that although image has the lowest ranking, it is a key in obtaining the other two. Had the junior senator from Massachusetts been overweight and bald, chances are he would never have inspired the public to elect him president, and most certainly the public perception of his importance would have been much different.

We hope to inform today's image-conscious male about developments in several key areas:

1. We will present compelling evidence in support of the importance of a handsome, masculine image. We hope to show, beyond question, that a handsome image improves every aspect of a man's life.
2. We will provide some cultural background to show how the perception of masculine image is constantly changing.
3. We will provide detailed information on many of the resources currently available to maximize your image.

The accumulation of this knowledge represents the leading edge in a science we term *Image Enhancement Technology*.

4. By using the science of Image Enhancement Technology, we demonstrate how you can transform your image and your life.

There are thousands of books, audio cassettes, and videotapes on success, motivation, and self-help, yet hardly a mention is made about the importance of image. We fill that void by providing an awareness of the vital role your image plays in obtaining professional and social success. The information contained here will give you an edge over other men who lack this knowledge.

1

The Importance of Your Image

A WORLD OF CHANGE

Most people, even the most intelligent among us, tend to resist change because they perceive it as a threat. There is nothing more sure than the fact that things are constantly changing and will continue to change. All any man over thirty has to do is to compare the world today with the world he knew when he was growing up. This comparison is even more drastic for those over the age of fifty.

Before the advent of today's mass media, men constructed an image of who they were through face-to-face interaction. Later we developed images from descriptions and pictures found in books, newspapers, and magazines. As the motion picture industry emerged, we enhanced our perception of the male image through the roles projected by actors on the silver screen. In the late 1940s and early 1950s the technology of television brought new images into our living rooms. The personalities on early television dramatically reinforced traditional beliefs about the strengths and weaknesses of men and women. Programs such as "Ozzie and Harriet," "Leave It to Beaver," and "The Donna Reed Show" portrayed men and women, husbands and wives performing their traditional duties. Of course, the man could not do the woman's job, nor could the woman do the man's. If the man was left at home alone to do any type of housework, he was sure to destroy the place. The message was obvious: men are incapable of taking care of themselves. The movie *Mr. Mom* was probably one of the last attempts to use this as a theme for entertainment. The women fared no better: the plots of "I Love Lucy" come to mind. Every time Lucy ventured out of the house and into any work environment, she botched it. Most of the plots of the show were centered around her quest to leave the house and get into show business or have a career. The message was obvious here as well.

The late 1950s and the 1960s brought a whole new glossary of terms and phrases into our vocabulary, including: "do your own thing," "love ins," "my own space," and "computers." The first appearance by the Beatles on "The Ed Sullivan Show" in 1963 had the whole country talking, not just about their revolutionary new sound but also about *their hair*. The image of the Beatles defied the prevailing standard that a man's hair should not cover his ears or his forehead. Within a year many young men had grown hair down to their shoulders and corporate executives, who previously had the short military look, now sported hair that covered their button-down collars. This change was viewed as a sign of decline by the "morality police," who decided that short hair was good and long hair was bad.

In the 1970s previously suppressed minority groups were using the power of the ballot box to obtain their piece of the American dream. Federally mandated programs such as the Equal Employment Opportunity Act gave birth to the quota system. The feminist movement had gained great momentum, spawning such national groups as the National Organization of Women (NOW) and an increasing number of the women in the United States were working outside the home and were also being elected to political office in greater numbers. More women were being placed in positions of responsibility, places that had previously been defined as only a man's job. Women were becoming bank presidents, stockbrokers, newscasters, and even sports reporters. As men and women became less dependent on each other and the need for two-income households increased, the divorce rate began to soar. Women were at last on the road to gaining parity with men in the workplace. The single, working, "liberated" woman began to express her new-found independence with a lifestyle that allowed for more than one sexual partner, another part of life previously accepted as reserved for men only. Society had moved out of the age of conformity and togetherness and into the age of disco, singles, and one-night stands.

The 1980s ushered in the "me" generation, fueled by mergers, takeovers, and corporate acquisitions. Greed was no longer a sin, it was an attribute: if you were not greedy, you were not thought to be motivated. A very popular saying was: "Life is a game. The one with the most toys wins." In the 1980s, while some were milking billions from the financial markets and corporate restructuring, hundreds of thousands of good, hard-working people lost their jobs. As men saw their livelihoods disappear, more women were forced to find work outside the home in order to save their homes and families. This added financial pressure caused an already high divorce rate to increase.

Many of the skills and crafts that had always insured a man's financial security were being rendered obsolete by new technology. To make things worse, along with the competition from abroad, the giant North American corporations became multinational, moving jobs off shore to gain the advantage of cheap foreign labor. It is interesting to note that many of the companies listed in the 1970 Fortune 500 no longer exist.

More men are now realizing that the skills they possessed, those special qualities that got the job done, are no longer required. Men need to move away from yesterday, out of their comfort zone, and adopt new attitudes, develop new skills, and realize that the traditional male image they grew up with is fading fast. Many of the traditional occupations and attitudes that defined the American man just forty years ago are racing toward extinction in the 1990s.

MASCULINE IMAGE AND TECHNOLOGY

The historic role of man as the hunter and provider has long since passed. Many men now find themselves increasingly confused and frustrated as they try to maintain their masculine identity. In this volume we intend to deal with the concept of the new emerging male image. We are not writing for men whose values and thinking are stuck in the past. Instead, you will learn about the growing importance of masculine image in this new age of exploding technology. It has been said that there have been more advances in technology during the past ten years than there had been since the beginning of time. The tremendous impact of these advances is accelerating the pace of cultural evolution so rapidly that any man who fails to recognize, accept, or appreciate the great changes that are occurring will be left behind. The comfortable little pockets of provincialism and their associated attitudes about how men should view themselves will disappear as our world continues to shrink under the power of technology.

Technology is changing our world and the way men and women live in it. All the business magazines and financial newsletters tell us that many of the accepted business practices advocated and implemented since the Second World War are no longer valid. To be competitive and successful in this new world market, we must change the way we manage our business. To be competitive and successful, we must apply an updated definition of who we are, recognizing the implications of the changes around us. One of the most significant changes in modern society is the importance of masculine image, which seems to be escalating with each new advance in technology.

THE CASTE SYSTEM OF IMAGE

The caste system in India was a hierarchical social stratification that classified and ranked human beings by specific categories. The lowest classification, the untouchables, was assigned to people believed to be of so little value that their mere touch defiled those of other classes. It was believed that the plight of these people was due to sins in a past life. The untouchables were deemed to be "unclean" and were made to live apart from the rest of society. When Mahatma Gandhi became leader of India, the caste system was legally abolished by the new constitution, but for many years the social separation continued.

While India's caste system was in effect, it dictated many facets of everyday life: what people could do, how they should dress, what they ate, and most particularly who they could associate with, even who they could marry. People's achievable level of success in life was predetermined by the caste into which they were born.

Although India's rigid caste system was officially abolished, it still exists in various forms today and similar stratifications can be found throughout world. Though its forms are much more subtle the effect can be just as brutal to those individuals upon whom it frowns. The caste system as we know it now is seldom talked about—it is the caste system of image.

The term "cast," in its more familiar usage, remains part of our language. One of its definitions is in the theatrical sense of assigning a certain role or part to an actor. In addition to their talent, actors are chosen for parts in plays or movies based on their physical appearance: their youth or age, their height, build, and other characteristics. A "casting" director knows that an audience expects certain characters to look a certain way. Lanky, boyish Jimmy Stewart developed his career playing an honest, all-American guy, while the short, stocky, squinting Edward G. Robinson became famous playing gangsters. In the old cowboy movies, the "good guy" usually wore a white hat and the "bad guy" usually wore a black one. Even today movie heroes are usually younger and good looking, while villains are often portrayed by someone who looks sinister. It is not surprising that, despite our claim that books shouldn't be judged by their covers, most of us tend to believe that we can determine a great deal about people based solely on the way they look.

The physical features and genetic characteristics assigned to each of us at birth sometimes find us playing a role in life we may not want. Fortunately, living in today's world, we can apply for another role but first we must recast our image to fit the desired part we hope to play. During this "recasting" process we must ask ourselves three important questions:

1. What is my present role in life?
2. What role do I want to play?
3. What do I have to do to get the role I want?

A SUCCESSFUL IMAGE

Depending on the circumstances, your description of a successful image will not always remain the same. For example, if you were contemplating investing money with a brokerage firm or some other financial institution, you may become uncomfortable if the person representing the broker dressed flamboyantly. Usually those who are entrusted with large monetary transactions are somewhat conservative and prudent and their attire reflects this. Expensive jewelry and $500 shoes could convey the message that the person is reckless and may not exercise the proper judgment to handle investment dollars efficiently. On the other hand an investment counselor who presents himself in a pinstripe, conservative suit and maybe a pair of rimless glasses is much more comforting. However, if you had decided to put the cares of the world aside and take a vacation cruise, you would not want to be greeted by a cruise director who looked like a stockbroker.

In Nazi Germany a successful image was represented by the tall, blond-haired,

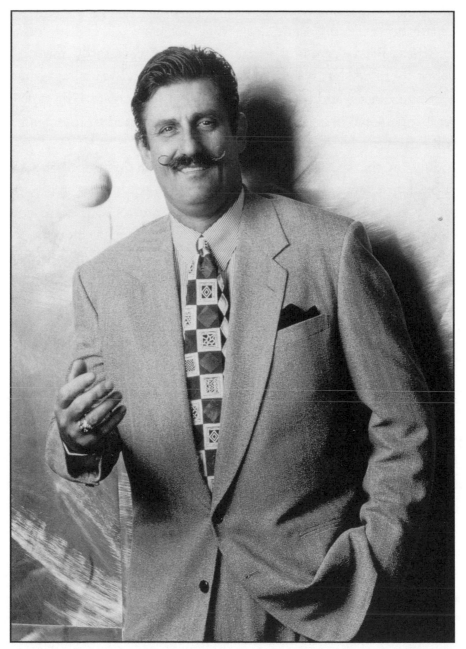

Hall of Fame professional baseball superstar Rollie Fingers enhanced his on-field athletic ability with a unique off-field image. (Photograph courtesy of Comb, Inc.—Just For Men Hair Color®)

blue-eyed man; however, this same image may not have been as successful in the jungles of Africa. By a successful image we do not necessarily mean that of a male model or a movie star, we are talking about *your* individual appearance, *your* individual circumstances, and the impression *you* wish to create. The type of image you project is a personal decision and should be constructed to meet *your* personal goals and objectives.

Depending on the specific situation at hand, your definition of a successful image is subject to change, but there are many basic truths that apply, regardless of the image you chose to project. These truths relate to your skin, your teeth, your eyes, your hair, your clothes, and much more. We do not focus on any specific image as the ideal one but, instead, we provide all men with valuable information on enhancement technology directed to the principles of a successful masculine image.

YOUR IMAGE

No doubt when you were young the question was often asked: "*What* do you want to be when you grow up?" The real question should have been: "*Who* do you want to be?" since *who* you are strongly determines *what* you project to the rest of the world. The perception others have of you is based largely on *what* they see.

A primary consideration in personal image development is how you perceive yourself and how you want to be perceived. The information we have to offer can make your desired self-perception (the way you wish you were) a reality. To attain the benefits of this book, you should prepare a wish list of all the things you want to change about your appearance. Before beginning your list, you should describe your major image objective. For example:

I want to look younger.

I want to look "hot."

I want to look more professional.

I want to look more masculine.

I want to look artistic.

I want to look powerful and influential.

I want to look like myself, only better.

As our title indicates, we want to share with you "The Secrets of a Successful Image." We hope that our effort will help you acquire the power to transform your image and become *who* you really want to be.

"What a man sees when he looks in the mirror can color the way he faces the world. Today, men are looking into a far different mirror than the one their fathers used. Contemporary men look at themselves with a kind but critical eye and they take action on the things they can change."

Ms. Anne York
Combe Incorporated

STARTING OVER

For many people there comes a point in life when everything seems to unravel. This may be the ending of a relationship, the loss of a job, or any number of things. It could be that you just wake up one morning and realize that your life is not what you want it to be and you recognize that changes have to be made. When reaching this point, logic often dictates that to get your life back in order you virtually have to start over. Starting over always involves change, and the nature of this change is intended to be self-improvement. Most of the current

Coauthor and professional model Anthony Chiappone. The information in this volume can change the way you look at yourself.

reference sources on personal self-improvement promote methods such as defining and pursuing your goals and objectives, by making lists of things you want to accomplish. All of these motivational techniques have merit but unfortunately, in many cases, they omit or discount a basic principle of human nature. These books or tapes outline principles on how to be a leader, how to influence people, how to build wealth and power, or how to develop and maintain a relationship but they usually fail to mention the importance of your appearance as a factor in reaching any of these objectives.

If you have reached that point in your life when you feel it is time to start over, before you evaluate your goals and objectives, perhaps you should first go to the mirror and evaluate your appearence.

Great emphasis has been placed on the way *you* react when in certain situations and circumstances, but the real key is the way *others* react to you. It is not reasonable or fair to indicate that the application of the rules of success work equally well for all individuals. It is not reasonable or fair to suggest that an overweight man has all of the same opportunities in life that a slimmer man has. A key factor in the attainment of success and happiness relates to that facet of human nature which deals with the impact of image. If some university were ever to offer a degree in the study of happiness and success, image enhancement would have to be at the top of the list of required courses.

2

Your Health

WHAT'S GOOD, WHAT'S BAD

If you do not maintain good health, all the self-help books on success, motivation, or self-improvement will have little meaning. Good health is the basic requirement for happiness and a full, rich life. We cannot talk about the details of image enhancement without first mentioning the basics of good health. A state of robust health is positively reflected in your image. Your health is your most important treasure, but as in the case of your image, your state of health should not become an obsession that takes precedence over everything else. Contemporary culture seems to be divided into two distinct camps; those whose lifestyle of substance abuse or poor diet reflects a complete disregard for their health, and those who are constantly preoccupied with matters concerning their health. Both of these groups are doing themselves a great disservice.

Today, we are being bombarded with misinformation about how to stay healthy. If we were to believe and follow the information found in some of the miracle diet books, it could make for a miserable and unhealthy life. Your personal health should always be a prime consideration but never an obsession. There is no single "magic bullet" that will guarantee everyone good health, but if there is one element that can contribute significantly to a state of robust health, it is a happy, positive attitude. Conversely, many people who are perpetually unhappy, stressed, or depressed often express a negative attitude and are more prone to an unhealthy lifestyle.

The following are some basic yet fascinating facts that we have learned over the years and now pass on to you.

THE FOUR ESSENTIAL FACTORS FOR LIFE AND HEALTH

Good health is one of the keys to a good life. With the exception of a fatal accident, an ongoing loss of health will ultimately result in a reduced quality of life. Often it is up to you whether your life is filled with exuberance or overwhelmed with stress and depression. Without an emphasis on good health, that image of yours will suffer.

The four components all of us need to sustain life are the same four items that can give us better health. In order of importance they are: *air, water, rest,* and *food.*

Air

No human being can live if he is deprived of air for more than ten minutes. The oxygen in the air sustains us. Our bodies are composed of billions of cells, each of which is nourished by oxygen. One of the main causes of premature aging, and many illnesses, is a lack of oxygen to the cells. When people become sick, they are often said to "lose their color," and become pale and bluish. This is one indication that their system is deprived of oxygen.

Inhaled oxygen builds red blood cells and purifies the blood that feeds every organ of the body. Wastes and poisons are eliminated by the lungs when they exhale. Every function of your body depends on breathing.

Deep Breathing

This is an ancient exercise many of us had to perform in grammar school gym classes. While standing with your feet about twelve inches apart and your arms and hands at your side, gradually rise up on your toes and raise your arms sideways to an overhead position, all the while breathing in deeply through your mouth. As you inhale, draw in your stomach as if you were trying to make it touch your backbone. After completely filling your lungs, exhale forcefully, but slowly, through your mouth, returning to the starting position. Repeat this exercise as many times as is comfortable for you.

The use of oxygen has saved the lives of millions of "oxygen-starved people" who have been near death because of respiratory or heart problems. One of the early treatments for "a run-down condition" was to spend time near the ocean, where the sea air could help revive health. The deep breathing exercise, performed daily, can eliminate stored toxins from your body, which will improve your overall health, vitality, and appearance.

Oxygen Technology

There are portable oxygen units available that you may wish to use. These units can be purchased at many medical supply stores without a prescription. They can be used as an energy booster to fight fatigue caused by an overload of carbon dioxide in your blood. Professional football players use portable oxygen units to replenish their energy. Caution should be exercised when using any type of oxygen unit since excessive oxygen intake could make you light-headed and might cause other physical problems such as fainting and blackouts.

How can an increased level of oxygen improve your image? Aerobic exercise or deep breathing increases the amount of oxygen carried by your blood, which has the positive effect of helping to impart physical vitality and a youthful, healthy glow to your skin.

Water

Studies indicate that humans cannot survive for more than a week without water. Like air, water is a source of support for plant and animal life. The average man's body contains about forty-five quarts of water, which constitutes about 92 percent of the volume of his blood and 98 percent of his other body fluids. The lack of adequate water intake can cause premature aging and wrinkled, dry skin. Failure to consume enough water will cause constipation, which many medical experts feel is a cause of illness in humans. It is now an accepted fact that a diet high in fiber promotes good health by encouraging regularity, which flushes waste and toxins from the body. The addition of six to eight, eight-ounce glasses of water daily will enhance the benefits of a high-fiber diet.

Like the cooling system in your car, water helps maintain your body temperature at 98.6°F. In addition, as we have stated, 92 percent of your blood, which supplies all the life-giving nutrition to every cell of our body, is water. The quality of your blood and urine may be directly affected by your intake of water.

Drink 6 to 8 glasses of water every day.

Public awareness regarding the deteriorating quality of tap water has created the relatively new industry of home water-processing units. There are basically two types of these units: those focusing on filtration and those emphasizing distillation. A decision to purchase one of these units may depend on where you live since the quality of drinking water varies from one geographic location to another. If you are already purchasing bottled water, switching to a distillation or filtration unit could pay for itself in less than a year.

Distillation Units

A distillation unit mimics the action of nature by taking water, evaporating it to gas (steam), and reconverting (condensing it) to water. During this process many chemicals and toxins are removed, yielding a more pure water. If you decide to drink distilled water, take a multivitamin/mineral supplement because some of the important organic matter we receive from water may be lost during the distilling process.

Filtration Units

Filtration units, such as those sold by NSA, remove many substances (e.g., chlorine and sulfur) but do not destroy the mineral content of drinking water. A good filtration unit will significantly enhance the taste and quality of the water you drink.

Rest

If a human being is deprived of sleep for more than a week the result can be fatal or at least emotionally debilitating. How much sleep do you need? Depending on your particular emotional and physical vitality, the average requirement could range from six to nine hours.

Many men think that the ability to work and play for long periods without sleep is an indication of their endurance. Some boast of working a double shift and then coming home to work in the garage all day. Yes, they may be tough, but over time this type of behavior could make them prime candidates for a coronary because constant physical or mental stress without the benefit of rest has an adverse effect on the body.

There is sleep and there is rest. Although many men may sleep eight or even nine hours a night, they do not know how to rest and relax. No matter how much you may enjoy your career, there should be a part of your life devoted to relaxation. Many men may experience a sense of guilt connected to relaxation. They feel compelled to justify their pleasure to themselves and to their buddies as something they had to do.

Consider this situation between George and Fred. One summer afternoon while relaxing in a lounge chair in his backyard, George hears his next-door neighbor Fred working on his house. Fred takes a break from his work and yells over the fence: "It must be nice. I wish I had the time to lay around like you." George looks up from his chair and says, "Why can't you?" Fred's puzzled look shows that he may well have realized that he was intentionally filling up every spare minute with some kind of a task. If he had a week off, it took him a week to paint the side of his house. George believes he must have a worklist prepared prior to every vacation.

Fred is a perfect neighbor. His lawn and house are always well kept. He spends every waking hour, with the exception of job commitments, working on his house. Certainly it is not George's place to say how others should relax, but looking back, George sure hopes Fred enjoyed these tasks, which took the place of his leisure time, because, you see, Fred died (from kidney failure brought on by high blood pressure) at the young age of thirty-eight, leaving a young wife and daughter.

Poor Fred was a "model husband," and along with concern for his job, his house, his car, his lawn, and the like, he obviously had concern for his family. Fred's life insurance paid his wife handsomely. Fred's wife did not remain a widow very long. Someone recently told George that she and her new husband took an extended honeymoon in Hawaii.

Adequate amounts of sleep, rest, and relaxation make for a long and healthy life. Depriving yourself of this important time to recharge will show on you in the form of poor muscle tone, nervous tension, the inability to handle stress, and diminished sexual vitality.

It's time to wake up and relax.

Sleep Technology

If you have a stress-related or physical disorder that interferes with your sleep, there are some options that can help specific problems and encourage a full, restful night's sleep. Along with improvements in the traditional mattress and box spring and the introduction of waterbeds, relaxation audiotapes to help you doze off, special multiposition contour beds, and form-fitting pillows can now be purchased to make your sleeping hours more restful. We wish to offer one suggestion that hardly falls into the category of technology but is very important: make sure the room you sleep in has good ventilation. If possible (weather permitting), open a window or be sure your air conditioning and heating units have good, clean air filtration systems.

How do sleep, rest, and relaxation affect your image? It does not require any medical knowledge to recognize when someone is affected by lack of sleep or is "stressed out." The signs are very easy to detect (e.g., dark circles and lines under the eyes and a general look of fatigue). It can also manifest itself in a slow, labored speaking voice and lethargic body movement.

Food

Ninety days is the longest recorded time anyone has ever survived without food. As you can see, food is the least important factor compared to air (oxygen), water, and sleep. Relative to your personal health and your image, food becomes a very important factor. In a very real sense "you are what you eat."

Unless you have been living in a cave for the past twenty years, you already know about the basics of a healthy diet. The only logic that applies to a sound diet is common sense and a few basics about nutrition. Fad diets that tell you to consume ridiculous combinations such as ten grapefruit and twenty-five glasses of water a day defy common sense. These diets appeal to desperate people who are willing to believe anything. In the bodyweight and bodybuilding section of this book we will list diet recommendations that are based on the most current nutritional information.

The information contained in most diet and nutrition books on the market today can be summed up in two sentences. Don't consume excessive amounts of fat, sugar, and caffeine. Try to eat lots of fresh vegetables, fresh fruit, and fiber.

Free Radicals

One of the more significant developments in the field of nutrition is the discovery of the action of antioxidants on human cells. Along with your blood, skin, and organs every fiber of nerve and muscle is made up of cells. Your very existence depends on your cells. Everything around you—the food you eat, the water you drink, even the air you breathe—contains destroyers of cells called free radicals, which chemically break down the protective barriers around the cells and over time cause illness and premature aging.

Research has shown that a daily intake of antioxidants, such as the combination of vitamins C, E, and Beta Carotene, serves to fight the action of free radicals. Even the recommended daily amount (RDA) of vitamin C (59MG), E (30IU), and Beta Carotene (no RDA) may be hard to obtain through your consumption of food because of food processing practices and overcooking. One way to insure that you are getting your daily requirement of antioxidants is to take one of the antioxidant formulas found in any drug or health food store.

Although there are many supplements and health foods we can purchase, the fact is that good health does not come in a bottle. In order to maintain your health you must be persistent, if not compulsive. Although many negative comments have been made about compulsive behavior, we wish to conclude this segment by stating the most important rule of good health: "If you wish to be healthy, you must become a compulsive moderate." Moderation in all aspects of your life is a major key to health. Some recent studies indicate that a person who has one alcoholic drink a day may be at less risk from heart attacks than those who abstain. Conversely, an individual who has six alcoholic drinks every day increases his risk of heart problems. Excessive consumption of fat has proven to be a cause of heart attacks but some circulatory and cardiovascular problems are now beginning to surface in individuals on extreme low fat diets.

It is not necessary to drink a gallon of vegetable juice or run ten miles a day to maintain your good health, in fact these types of extreme measures could cause health related problems.

3

Image Enhancement Technology

THE LOGIC OF IMAGE

In the 1993 movie *The Man Without a Face* actor Mel Gibson plays a former teacher who was badly burned and scarred in an auto accident. During the summer he lives on a resort island in New England. His deformed and scarred face was the focal point for residents' speculation about his past. Was he a killer? Maybe a child molester?

None of these stories proved to be true, and none of the people who told them ever knew or even talked to the former teacher. The stories were based strictly on the fact that his face was mutilated. If you look horrible then you must do horrible things. In the movie adaption of Edgar Allan Poe's *The Raven* actor Boris Karloff tells costar Bela Lugosi "Ugly men do ugly things," and whether we admit it or not most of us tend to think that way. To many people the real horror of serial killer Ted Bundy was that he was so good looking. He seemed nice and clean cut, like the guy next door.

The motion picture *10* got its name from the story line in which Bo Derek's character is given a rating of ten, which meant she was perfect. This motion picture started a trend, and today it is very common for men to rate women on a numerical scale of one through ten.

The truth is that all of us, consciously or unconsciously, assign an image rating to people we meet. We rate others and they rate us; often this rating has nothing to do with sexuality. But it can mean the difference in getting a much sought after job or continuing to circle the classifieds; in getting that promotion or being passed over.

Regardless of the occasion—be it business or social—when others meet you for the first time they will rate you based on what they see. In a split second they will develop a definite opinion about who you are. Some of the factors that become part of this on-sight opinion are your current economic status, your education, your background, your intelligence, and even your integrity. Although this opinion about you has been formed "in the blink of an eye" it could take months of personal interaction to undo any negative first impression you might have made. A current shampoo commercial isn't far off the mark when it concludes, "You never get a second chance to make a good first impression."

The establishment of the Intelligence Quotient (I.Q.) scale and testing has allowed us to measure and describe the intelligence of a person as below-average, average, or above-average intelligence. It is possible that these three categories may not be adequate since the people on the low end of the average category are significantly less likely to attend college or have success in a profession than those who place toward the top of the category. Most I.Q. testing was done in our early grammar school years and the definition of "average" was probably established to embrace the majority of the students, making them feel equal even though this truly was not the case.

Let's assume that there is a computer scanning device that could rate men based strictly and solely on the way they looked; let's call the rating produced by this computer an Image Quotient (I.Q.). Let's assume that this computer rated men using the same numerical system that men now use to rate women.

1–2   below average

3–7   average (Although they are both within the average range, would you rather date a woman rated as a 3 or one rated a 7?)

What if men were rated using the same system they now use to rate women? What would your Image Quotient be? (Photograph courtesy of Sharon Barber)

8   above average

9   great

10   perfect

Let's assume this computer scan could not detect any makeup on the man being tested. In other words, Mel Gibson playing his character in *The Man without a Face* would score a 1, but Gibson as himself would probably score a 9 or 10.

How would you score your own Image Quotient?

As in the case of intelligence there is a significant difference between the men on the low end of the average image quotient rating and those placing toward the high end. Where is the cut-off point at which your looks become unimportant? Where is that point of "average," where better-looking becomes unimportant? That point does not exist.

We know that people on the high end of average intelligence are apt to do better than those on the low end. This is also true in the case of image.

If the mythical image quotient computer actually existed and if you feel you are on the low end of average, we believe that if you decide to consider seriously our advice on image transformation, it could raise your image quotient 2 to 6 points.

It has been said that the average person could never imagine how different this world looks through the eyes of a multimillionaire. Along with the obvious material advantages a millionaire possesses, his life is filled with courtesy and respect from nearly everyone with whom he has occasion to come into contact. Using a similar analogy, a man of below-average appearance could never imagine how the world of opportunity looks through the eyes of those men who are above average in appearance. Doesn't it make sense to take all possible steps to maximize your personal Image Quotient when the opportunity presents itself?

A man of below-average appearance could never imagine how the world of opportunity looks through the eyes of a man whose appearance is above average. (Photograph courtesy of The Sinclair Institute, Chapel Hill, North Carolina)

IMAGE ENHANCEMENT TECHNOLOGY

Computer-based technologies such as fiber optics, CD-ROM, and micro chips are recent breakthroughs, with far-reaching implications. The technologies of bio-chemistry and genetic engineering offer the promise of eliminating devastating illnesses such as cancer and neuromuscular disease. In the past one hundred years, technologies such as the automobile, the airplane, electricity, motion pictures, television, central heating, air conditioning, and food processing have radically altered (and will continue to affect) the way we live. One example of this is that during the past twenty-five years there has been a great population shift from the northeastern to the southern states. This migration to the south would not have occurred if it were not for the technology of air conditioning.

In recent years there have been many advances in the science that deals with enhancing a man's image. Today, we now have reached the point at which all men have the ability to maximize their personal image by taking advantage of Image Enhancement Technology (IET). Viewed in its broadest possible context, IET would encompass all available components of a current technology that can enhance masculine image. The specifics of this technology are outlined in detail in the upcoming chapters. These will include innovations designed to enhance your hair, your skin, your weight, your height, and your face and complexion.

4

Your Nonvisual Image

YOUR ACTIONS, YOUR IMAGE

Although the secrets of a successful image are focused on matters pertaining to the sense of sight and how people react to visual messages, we need to point out that there are significant aspects of developing a successful image that have nothing whatever to do with physical appearance. Your actions, as well as your senses of hearing and of smell are powerful image enhancers in their own right. Let's consider some of these nonvisual aspects of your image.

One of the newer buzz phrases is the term "body language." Those who profess to be experts in the study of body language say that specific physical motions or gestures signal specific emotions. Here are some examples of body-language translations:

Arms folded across the chest indicates a protective position.

A slouching posture indicates a feeling of defeat.

A clenched fist indicates aggression or anger.

Rubbing your eyes is a sign of stress.

Your physical image must be matched by your actions and your etiquette. No doubt you have met someone who appeared to be sharp and polished, but after a few minutes you realized that he was a jerk. The reason for your quick change of opinion was the way he spoke and/or the way he acted. The man who is ultimately successful possesses a respect for himself and others: you may call it being a gentleman, having manners, or understanding proper etiquette. Whatever you choose to call this type of demeanor, it should be an implicit part of your successful image.

One of the most dashing figures in literature and on the motion picture screen was secret agent 007, James Bond. The real attraction of the James Bond character centered on his diversity: his rugged yet sophisticated approach. He was capable of blowing up an enemy installation and fearlessly driving his car at breakneck speeds over twisting mountain roads, yet he had impeccable manners and a debonair persona. He appreciated good food and drink (his martinis were shaken, not stirred). James Bond knew how to introduce himself to women, making sure they remembered him: "The name is Bond, James Bond." He was feared and respected by men, and loved by women the world over.

James Bond is a fictional character, but the type of man he represents is the epitome of masculinity. At the extreme end of the male persona, the tough guy macho image may be just an attempt to cover up a self-perception of inadequacy or a means to gain recognition within certain male-dominated ethnic or economic groups.

One secret of a successful image is to cultivate a genuine sensitivity toward the feelings of others and to your surroundings. Here are a few tips:

- If you are seated when introduced to someone, stand up.

- Pay extra attention when being introduced to a person of importance, or to a woman.

- When you shake hands your grip should send a message of sincerity and confidence.

On a Date

- When dining out with a woman or with business associates, dress in a manner appropriate to the occasion and the restaurant.

- As the woman leaves or returns to the table, always stand and hold her chair. When you are being seated in a restaurant, your female companion should follow the maitre'd or headwaiter: he will seat her, and you will take the seat next to her. If there is no maitre d' on duty, lead the woman to your table and seat her.

"Ladies before gentlemen" used to be the customary rule. Opening a door or holding a chair for a woman was accepted practice. Showing respect for women is a male tradition passed down from generation to generation. Many of these traditions are now labeled sexist because some view such acts as chauvinistic, but the majority of women still want to feel special, and they get that feeling from a man who acts like a gentleman.

Meeting People

If you wish to meet someone, always introduce yourself before you ask the other person's name. After the introductions are complete, tell the other person a little about yourself, but don't be long-winded about it; this will normally make the person more comfortable with you. Try to establish a common ground and talk about things that your new acquaintance appears to like to talk about. Most people enjoy talking about themselves, but by showing a little interest in the other person you can learn a great deal about him or her. The more you listen, the more your new acquaintance will trust you.

Some men experience difficulty approaching and meeting others, especially someone for whom they feel a romantic attraction. This reluctance is usually considered shyness, but is often due to some real or perceived image problem. The answers to many of the image questions are given within these pages. For those men who are not shy, we wish to offer some advice. If you approach someone to whom you are attracted and are not receiving positive feedback, don't push. It is best to excuse yourself politely. Pressure will only raise the defense shields of the person you approach. Remember, people often want what they can't have, so play it smart.

Poor Posture and How to Correct It

You probably remember hearing this common admonishment given by a teacher or by your parents: "stand up straight." You should always attempt to stand and walk so you don't look like you're involved in a constant struggle with gravity. Poor posture can make you look fatigued or defeated and it can also make you look older. The following are a few tips that can help you recognize and correct problems regarding posture.

Analyze Your Posture

Check the bottoms of your shoes: are either the heels or soles worn down more on one side than on the other? As in the case of uneven tire wear, when the wheels of your car are not properly aligned, uneven wear on your shoes is an indication that you are not walking properly.

Do you constantly suffer from soreness in your back, neck, and shoulders? When you slouch or stand stoop-shouldered, your poor posture compresses vertebrae and creates muscle spasms.

Is your breathing irregular or uncomfortable? Although breathing problems often signal some serious condition, it may just be a result of poor posture that places pressure on your diaphragm.

It is vital that you develop an awareness of your posture without looking stiff or ramrod straight. To help you find your ideal posture, stand with your heels, buttocks, shoulders, and head touching a wall. Take a deep breath and relax while maintaining the four points of contact. As you walk away from the wall your body weight should now feel centered.

Your midsection or waist is your center of gravity; we recommend consistent abdominal exercise to strengthen the muscles in this area. It is interesting to note that many lower back problems are simply the result of weak abdominal muscles, which can be made stronger through exercise. Firm stomach muscles provide increased support to the lumbar area of the back.

Body language sends loud and strong messages to others, so walk, stand, and move with confidence. Always be aware of your body movement and your gestures.

It is not unusual for parents who want their children to become involved in some type of activity to send their sons to a sports camp and their daughters to a dance school. But if only females learn to dance, who are they suppose to dance with? Many parents do not realize that if they sent their sons to dance school far more boys would become much better athletes. Dancing requires skill, timing, and coordination. Most professional sports fans would be very surprised if they were to see the skills of their favorite superstar on the dance floor.

Dancing is an important factor in most cultures. Anyone studying the culture of another ethnic group will want to learn about their traditional dances. Since the beginning of civilization humankind has used the vehicle of the dance to express both happiness and sorrow. The combination of a fine dinner followed by dancing can constitute a perfect evening. Unfortunately many men miss a very pleasurable experience and lack an important social skill because they cannot dance. The art of dancing was a required skill in the royal courts of Europe and even in colonial America. In the United States the social aspects of dancing extended from the barn dances of the Wild West to the jazz clubs of the Roaring Twenties. Somewhere along the way a good many men have come to believe that learning how to dance is not worth the effort. How many times have you seen couples at social occasions who just sit at their table all night while the woman looks on with envy at the couples on the dance floor. Sometimes women become so bored that they dance with each other.

We were told by one woman: "I can tell the way a man will be in bed by the way he moves on the dance floor." The movement of dancing can be more seductive than conversation. But why don't more men dance? In researching this question we were told that men are afraid they might appear unmasculine, foolish, or out of control; ironically, exactly the opposite is true. The description of a "ladies' man" will usually include the ability to "sweep a woman off her feet" on the dance floor. At both social or business gatherings the ability to dance well to all types of music—from slow ballads to upbeat salsa—is a true mark of sophistication.

If you can't dance you are depriving yourself of a world of fun times and opportunity. Forget about come-on lines such as "What's your sign?" or "Do you come here very often?" or "Haven't we met somewhere before?" The magic question that may have started more relationships than any other is "Would you like to dance?"

YOUR SENSES

What Are People Hearing from You, and How Do You Sound to Others?

Research has proven that many functions of your body can be altered by hearing various sounds. Some of the hot items on the market today are relaxation audiotapes containing sounds of nature such as waves breaking against the shore or a soft rain. It has been demonstrated through controlled tests that these sounds can slow a fast pulse thereby bringing down an elevated blood pressure. Similarly, many people are eased by classical music or soft instrumental recordings. If encouraging movement is the goal, then, for many, loud dance music starts feet moving and heartbeats racing.

It should come as no surprise that sound is used in many venues to alter human behavior. From "elevator music" to lullabies, from protest songs to advertising jingles, sound adds immeasurably to the way we perceive the world and each other.

The sound of your voice is part of your image. Many acting careers were ruined when motion pictures converted from silent films to talkies. John Gilbert was one of the major romantic leading men of the silent era, but when he appeared in his first talking movie his high, squeaky voice proved to be his undoing. Other actors with great speaking voices, such as the Barrymore brothers (John and Lionel), made the transition and became superstars. Unusual voices such as those of W. C. Fields, Groucho Marx, Marlon Brando, James Cagney, Jimmy Durante, and many others helped make them stars. Today the entertainment industry employs high-paid professionals to do "voice overs" for cartoons, commercials, and motion pictures. The various unique sounds of the human voice can communicate a range of moods from comedy to tragedy.

Have you ever heard someone say, "I thought he was a sharp guy until he opened his mouth?" At first the assumption might be that the person being talked about was saying things that were less than intelligent, but it also could be a reaction to the sound or rhythm of his voice. Any man with a high-pitched voice or a speech impediment is at a definite disadvantage both socially and professionally. Some people make a decision about who you are based on how you sound. Then of course there is the regional accent. A New York City accent can generate mistrust in some parts of the south, while a thick southern accent might find you labeled a hillbilly in some of the northern states. Many people in radio and television work very hard to eliminate regional speech inflections that could be viewed negatively when seeking employment in a nationwide market.

Does Your Voice Help or Hurt Your Image?

A few years ago, coauthor Anthony Chiappone was visiting a friend. Earlier in the day he left a message on his friend's answering machine and later that same day he heard his message played back through the recorder. When Anthony heard the sound of his own voice, he could not believe it. He never realized he talked so fast. Since that day Anthony has diligently worked on slowing down and improving the quality of his speaking voice.

If you're not sure about how the sound of your voice affects others, purchase a high-quality tape recorder and begin taping your end of telephone conversations or (with everyone's permission) tape your casual conversations at home. Play these tapes back and critique your own voice. You can listen to an "accepted" ideal voice just by turning on your television set to a network news program. News anchors like Dan Rather, Tom Brokaw, Peter Jennings, Ted Koppel, and others possess what's thought to be an ideal masculine speaking voice. Attitudes are changing on this issue with the popularity of cultural pluralism or multiculturalism, which has, to some extent, broadened the acceptable range of voice patterns.

The tone and rhythm of your voice can communicate confidence or fear, happiness or depression, enthusiasm or disinterest, friendliness or hostility. Along with your physical image, your voice can generate a multitude of impressions in others. Strive to become conscious not only of *what* you say, but *how* you say it. If you feel your voice does not compliment your overall image, work to change it by using some of the techniques recommended here, or by consulting a speech therapist. There are any number of professionals who specialize in neutralizing accents and perceived imperfections in speech.

In the early 1900s, there was a poor boy named Archibald Leach living in the industrial town of Bristol, England. When he was nine years old his mother was committed to a mental institution, leaving the young boy alone with his father, who worked as a tailor. Working for pennies as a street performer, Archibald Leach acquired skills as an acrobat and ultimately became associated with the Pender acrobatic troupe that had scheduled appearances in the United States. After the troupe completed its engagements in America, Leach decided not to return to England. His dream was to become a movie star in Hollywood. British actors were a hot item in Hollywood, and he wanted to cash in on this trend. In order to earn enough to make his trip to tinsel town, he got a job on the pier at Coney Island walking on stilts with sandwich board advertising for a local restaurant. He also sold men's neckties and handkerchiefs at a small concession on the pier.

Leach knew his chances of making it in the movies were remote since he lacked any semblance of culture or breeding, traits so evident in English actors. He had virtually no education and this deficit was magnified by a heavy cockney accent. Archibald Leach changed his appearance and worked for more than a year on his voice, trying to imitate the sophisticated British upper-class accent. He transformed his rough working-class mannerisms to those of a man of ultimate sophistication.

As the story goes, after he arrived in Hollywood, Leach was spotted by Mae West who, upon seeing this handsome young man, said, "If this guy can talk he will be a star." One thing Leach could do was talk. In his attempt to transform his cockney accent, he developed a speaking voice that was uniquely his own. His fabricated accent was unlike anything ever heard on a movie soundtrack. He invented his image, his personality, and even his speaking voice. By transforming his total image, Archibald Leach invented the whole new persona we now know as Cary Grant.

The Sound of Your Name

In the past, during periods of increased immigration to the United States, many Europeans changed or shortened their last names when they arrived at Ellis Island for processing: Robinowicz became Robbins and Martino became Martin. In a country where the establishment was composed of Anglo-Saxon Protestants, a "foreign"-sounding name could be a handicap to advancement, initially for themselves but later for their children. At one point coauthor Richard Derwald was considering a job offer with a major company in Vermont. A good, well-meaning friend suggested that before he moved to Vermont, Richard should consider changing his name. This suggestion came as a bit of a surprise to Richard since he did not see anything wrong with Richard Joseph Derwald. His friend's suggestion was that Richard Americanize his European name (Derwald means "the forest" in German), so the friend proposed that Richard translate his name to English, hence Richard Forest. The friend also suggested that Richard make up a first initial, drop his middle name, and become H. Richard Forest. Looking back at this suggestion, it makes much more sense today than it did at the time. In many situations H. Richard Forest would have a distinct advantage over Richard Derwald.

Upon hearing a person's name we immediately conjure up an image. What image comes to mind when you hear names like Rufas, Mario, Stanley, or Myron? In addition to possibly identifying an ethnic background, your name also carries stereotypical images. The name Percy may convey the image of a sissy while the name Norbert is often linked to a nerd or egghead. Bob, John, or Jake might be viewed as highly masculine, while Lance, Tad, or Brad could find us recalling the yuppie days of the 1980s.

Today we are seeing a change in places like Dade County, Florida, where Spanish is now a second "official" language. For the first time in the history of our melting-pot society, a new wave of residents has persevered, incorporating their native language into our changing culture. A Spanish surname could now be an advantage when applying for a position, especially with the government or civil service.

Your name is part of your identity. Many African Americans are now dropping their American (slave) names, and are taking on African names. They are doing this to reestablish what they feel is a lost identity. Along with their new African names, many have also modified their style of clothes to give them even more of a sense of self.

Sometimes the name/image association works in reverse and a person is given a nickname that to those who assign it, confers his image. Children often assign nicknames to their playmates: one boy may get the nickname Rocky because of his brash manner while another might be called Red because of his hair color. The image makers in Hollywood have known and manipulated the connection between name and image for years. In the fifties, movie stars emerged named Rock Hudson and Tab Hunter. Using one "grabber" name has proved to be very successful in defining the images of recording artists and other personalities, beginning with Fabian and Dion up to Madonna, Cher, Prince, and Fabio.

The sound of a name can bring to mind a variety of mental images; for example,

Who do you think is better looking, Elmer or Lance?

Who do you think is more serious, Leroy or Akeeme?

Who do you think is smarter, Rufus or Scott?

The sound of your name is important.

Generally speaking, no one will ever love you more than your mother, but she may have unknowingly harnessed you with a handicap. If you are uncomfortable with your name, or feel that it neither compliments your image nor serves your best interests, you may wish to consider a change. You can informally change your first name by simply telling people the new name you wish to use: for example, "Just call me Ted," or whatever first name you have chosen. Along with the prospect of offending some of your family members, changing your last name is a rather complex legal procedure involving formal changes to records such as social security history as well as your driver's license and credit cards. Changing your last name is not an overwhelming task, as is shown by the many women who take their husbands name when they marry, and the modern practice of couples combining their last names in a hyphenated manner.

Remember, your image is determined by a total package of factors, which includes your name.

The Smell of Success: Understanding Fragrances and How They Affect Your Image

Powerful physical and emotional responses can be evoked by your sense of smell. The olfactory sense can make you feel sick or incredibly aroused; it can bring back long forgotten memories, make you hungry, or stimulate sexual urges.

When the tomb of King Tutankhamen was unearthed in 1922, over three millennia after his elaborate burial, the aroma of potent fragrances lingered in the king's ornate perfume bottles. Today's billion-dollar men's fragrance industry is still relatively new, with almost half of the purchases of men's fragrances still being made by women. Because the use of cologne is relatively new to men, many of you need to understand some basic facts that most women have come to learn over the years.

- Something that smells good to others at ten o'clock in the evening may not have the same effect at nine o'clock in the morning.

- As in the case of vitamins, if a little is good, more is not necessarily better.

- The key word in using any fragrance is to be *subtle*; your fragrance should not linger in a room twenty minutes after you have leave.

- Your body chemistry can determine how a specific fragrance will smell on you. The same fragrance does not react the same way on every person.

- Your sense of taste is dependent on your sense of smell; an overpowering cologne could ruin a good dinner.

You should know that fragrances have three phases:

1. The initial scent you receive with the first sniff.

2. The main body of the fragrance and its principal aromatic theme.

3. The element of the fragrance that may linger after you have left a room.

The women of the nineties want their men to look good *and* smell good. (© Mike Pecorino)

The cologne you use is a matter of personal taste. Many men feel that their selection of a certain cologne is part of creating their individual trademark. The following is a short guide to the general categories of fragrances currently available for men.

Green: Getting its name not from its color but rather from its outdoorsy, "wooded-glade" type freshness. This group of fragrances often simulates a combination of herbs, ferns, and oakmoss. The use of green fragrances seems to be more appropriate during the winter months and in colder climates.

Citrus: This group of fragrances usually simulates accents of lemon, mandarin orange, lime, and other citrus fruit elements. Because of their clean, sharp scent, citrus fragrances are most popular during the summer months and in warmer climates.

Spicy: These simulate accents that include cinnamon, ginger, cloves, vanilla, and carnation. Spicy fragrances are usually stronger, longer lasting, and are therefore more appropriate for use in the evening hours.

Oriental: These heavier, exotic scents can include blends of sandalwood, patchouli, and musk. Oriental fragrances should be used with discretion during the day.

When shopping for a new cologne it is important that you allow the scent being tested to develop on your skin. This will require only three or four minutes and will give you the true scent combined with your individual body chemistry. It is also important not to test too many scents at one time. This will defeat your goal to find the cologne that is just right for you.

Your choice of fragrance can be an important image decision because it affects how others experience you and how you feel about yourself.

5

Masculine Image

BEING A MAN: SURFACE VERSUS SUBSTANCE

Is appearance more important than character or intelligence? Is *how* you look more important than *who* you are, or does how you look help to determine who you are? Although spiritual and intellectual people are usually at odds on most subjects, there is one viewpoint they both share: the worth of a human being is measured by inner substance and not by outer appearance.

To prove his point, the spiritual man may join some group where members shave their heads and wear loose, flowing robes; the intellectual may wear mismatched clothes or forget to comb his hair. Although the average man is not this extreme in his belief that substance counts the most, he may not comprehend the impact that image could be having on his life.

Personal image is a cornerstone of success in the sales profession. Regardless of the career you choose, if you are to succeed in either your personal life or your career, you must be able to sell yourself. Your personal image is a strong selling tool.

When combined with other attributes such as education, motivation, talent, ability, or skill, image can often be a deciding factor in determining your degree of success.

THE POWER OF MASCULINE IMAGE

To a great extent both men and women adopt a physical persona. Generally speaking, each group creates a visual representation of who it thinks it is, or, more often, who it wants to be. This representation is a package consisting of hairstyle, mode of dress, developed or acquired speech patterns, and body language. This representation may extend to members' vehicle types and their home decor.

It is obvious that all of us do not have the same ideal image. Let's look at a few of today's prevailing stereotypical masculine images.

The Yuppie

Sporting a short, conservative hairstyle, he "dresses for success" wearing conservative-cut suits; button-down, broadcloth shirts; an appropriate tie; and wing-tip shoes. His ideal car is a BMW or some equally expensive model.

The Blue-Collar Guy

He has medium-to-long hair and prefers denim shirts, blue jeans, and cowboy boots. He likes to drive a pick-up truck.

The White-Collar Man

He prefers a traditional hairstyle, tends to wear clothes stocked by discount chain stores, and drives an affordable car.

The Biker

Members of this group run the gamut from shaved heads to very long hair. They prefer leather jackets and biker boots. Their ideal vehicle is a Harley Davidson.

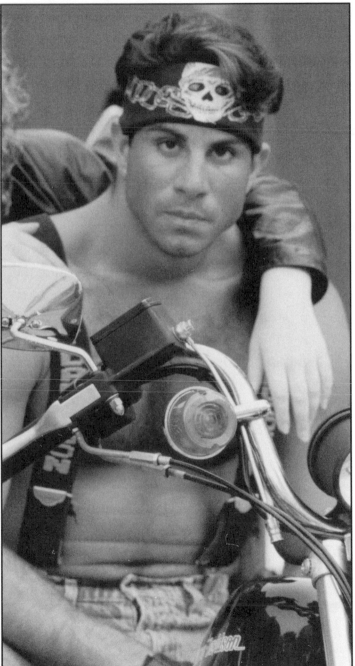

Is he a yuppie or a biker? Either way, you are the architect of your image. (Photograph courtesy of Anthony Ventura, © Jim Bush)

Now reread the descriptions of the images as listed above. Note that none of these relate to any inherited genetic or physical characteristics. Each describes superficial aspects that any member of any of the groups could change at will, especially clothes and hairstyle. Think about it: none of these characteristics are part of the man himself; they are only a visual manifestation of that individual's self-perception. To a great extent we are the architects of our own image. We choose an image and are guided by its characteristics.

Now suppose we switched the clothes and the hairstyle of the yuppie group and a person from the biker group, and forced them to maintain this image for one year. What effect do you think this mandated image switch would have on each individual? Based on human nature it is possible that over a period of time, each person would tend to acquire the values and mannerisms of the other group.

Picture yourself driving a beat-up, rough-riding, early-'70s-model car with rust and missing bumpers. How do you feel driving down the street? When you stop at an intersection you will probably look straight ahead not wanting to make eye contact with those crossing or those in the car next to you. Although this car is only a mechanical device that in no way has any real connection to you as a person, at the time you are driving it another person's perception of who you are could be negative because it is human nature to make an instant judgment based on what is seen.

Now picture yourself in a brand new Mercedes. What happens when you pull up to an intersection? Do you sit taller trying to catch the eye of people around you while flashing a smug smile at the guy next to you in an older car? For added effect you may even pick up your cellular telephone. The Mercedes may only be borrowed or rented but you experience that feeling of self-worth and importance. Few would disagree that when something makes us *look good*, it makes us *feel good*.

Once you park either car, get out, and walk away, you have lost a prop, a positive or negative image-maker. Without this prop you may well make a completely different impression on passersby as you walk down the street. Truly ours is a world of created impressions.

IMAGES OF POWER

Throughout history material objects have always been used as props to support the masculine image. This has been true from the days of ancient Rome when a man's power was demonstrated by how many horses he had in front of his chariot or how many slaves he had in his household. Today one sign of a man's success is how many horses he has under his hood. The Greek tale of Narcissus tells of a young man who fell in love with his own reflection. As a result of this obsession with his own physical appearance, Narcissus so admired his own beauty that he failed to eat and thus starved to death. Today an external form of narcissism can be found in men who collect objects that identify them with a specific desired image. This type of man is always eager to take you on a tour of his house. He may show you his polished gun collection in the game room, or his trophy room, or take you on a tour of the garage to see his newest power tools or muscle car.

Down through the centuries many rich and powerful men have attempted to enhance and immortalize their image through works of art. In the reception area of many Fortune 500 companies or major financial institutions it is not uncommon to see large oil paintings of former chairmen of the board. These paintings usually reflect some "artistic license" favoring their subjects.

Evidence of man's desire to immortalize his image ranges from the statues of King Tut, found in the Egyptian pyramids, to French Emperor Napoleon, with both paintings and statues of his famous pose. Even today, successful men may commission a sculptor to enhance and immortalize their image in carved stone or a bronze casting.

As demonstrated by his collection of wooden false teeth, George Washington understood the importance of image. The familiar likeness of Washington that we see on a one-dollar bill was taken from an oil portrait. While sitting for the portrait, Washington stuffed small pieces of cloth into the lower jaw region of his mouth squaring out his jaw line, giving his face a more authoritative appearance.

IMAGE AND THE MEDIA

A rather amusing incident occurred recently on a local television station. One of the anchors introduced a story and the appropriate videotape was started, but somewhere in the middle of the video the audio continued as the video switched back to the anchor who was in the process of having his makeup retouched. We all know that television personalities wear makeup for the cameras, but many people do not realize the tremendous emphasis the industry places on image. Now some may say, "Who cares what people look like when they are reporting about a major world problem?" The answer is, everyone. Studies of television viewers show that we all like to hear the news of the day from someone who looks intelligent, attractive, and informed, someone with a look of knowledge and concern. Network executives have known for years that (even though the same story is being aired) the audience tends to perceive the news it hears as being more accurate and complete when delivered by people who look (and speak) a certain way. This is why stations change their anchor people in an attempt to improve their ratings. This image requirement also exists for sportscasters and weather persons. In the case of the latter, even though the same source is used, namely, the national weather service, we tend to believe that even a weather forecast is more accurate when reported by someone who "looks right."

IMAGE AND POLITICS

When it comes to selecting local, state, and national leaders, we like to believe that we vote strictly on the candidates' positions on key issues, but this is not always true. The classic example of this remains the 1960 presidential candidate debate between Massachusetts Senator John F. Kennedy and Vice-President Richard

M. Nixon. It is the opinion of most political experts that this was the night Nixon lost the election.

Millions of people who watched television that evening were swayed by the startling visual contrast between the two candidates. Nixon had a brooding face with rather heavy jowls and drooping eyes with dark circles. He also had a very heavy beard making him appear as though he needed a shave. His image on television was almost sinister. To compound this problem, Nixon was just getting over a case of the flu, so he was weakened and rundown. His ailing condition caused him to break out in a sweat during the telecast. According to most published reports regarding that evening, Nixon did not take all the necessary steps to insure that his appearance would be a visual match for his opponent.

Senator John F. Kennedy, although basically an attractive man, had suffered from a back problem. He was on medication, which sometimes caused his face to look puffy and bloated. Kennedy's rise in politics was engineered by his father, Joseph Kennedy, a man who understood the importance of image and who was involved with the motion picture industry for many years. The night of the debate John F. Kennedy made use of subdued makeup to improve his image. As a result, he looked like the young, handsome, brilliant leader the country was longing for. Many people who watched the debate were moved more by what they saw than what they heard. Experts contend that if the debate had been aired only on radio, Nixon would have been the clear winner. In fact, many people who heard the debate only on the radio declared Nixon the winner.

Richard Nixon died in April 1994. According to Peter Jennings of ABC News, Nixon was quoted as saying, "I lost the debate with Kennedy because of poor lighting and poor makeup." Here is a case where major national and international issues may have been overshadowed by something as basic as makeup. Physical image influenced the public's perception of two men and this perception changed the history of the world.

The incident of the Kennedy/Nixon debate is really not an extreme example of image and politics. As a result of polio, President Franklin D. Roosevelt could not walk unassisted and was generally confined to a wheelchair. The American public was never really aware of the extent of his limitations. Since these were the days before television, the only way the general public was able to see national celebrities or politicians was at the movie theaters in newsreels or in newspapers. Prior to making any public speeches, President Roosevelt was propped up to simulate a standing position. It was only after he was placed in this standing position that the newsreel cameras were allowed to roll. This staging was necessary during the early period of the Second World War, when the country and the world needed the image of a strong leader.

Today, with the advent of expanded television coverage, image is probably one of the most important factors in determining the outcome of an election. It has been rumored that both Paul Newman and Robert Redford have been contacted by the major political parties to run for public office. In 1992 the Democratic party had Bill Clinton and Al Gore, while some believe that the Republican party is grooming Dan Quayle and Jack Kemp for 1996. Any of these four individuals would qualify for a role on a soap opera or a feature movie. Virtually the same success criteria apply to both politicians and actors as well as most positions of success. If anyone has doubts that image and acting skills are transferable to the political arena, let's not forget a man by the name of Ronald Reagan.

The images of these world leaders—Kennedy, Roosevelt, and Reagan—were partially created by press agents and public relations people. But the main ingredient had to be their own personal efforts. We are the artists of our lives and have the ability to develop and improve our individual image; in doing so, we have the means to improve every aspect of our lives.

IMAGE AND ENTERTAINMENT

It is a given that the entertainment world is completely image based, and the image must coincide with the entertainment being presented. The Rolling Stones have been called "the world's greatest rock and roll band." Assuming that their music was exactly the same, do you believe that the Stones would have enjoyed their great success if lead singer Mick Jagger had had a round moon face and a body to match? The on-stage physical persona of Jagger, Keith Richards, and all the members of this group suggests that they are "street wise bad boys." This carefully orchestrated image may be the greatest contributing factor to their success. Successful rock group legends such as ZZ Top and the Grateful Dead have also established uniquely identifiable images. All of these groups have created successful non-traditional images.

Large numbers of aspiring young musicians work weeks and months making demo tapes to send to the major record companies. Many believe that if they have a great song or a "brand new sound," the record companies will recognize it and give them a big recording contract. This usually does not happen, and television is a reason. During an interview, a popular singer said that while attending a meeting at a major record company the question of new talent came up. One of the people at this meeting had a cassette tape of a new vocalist he wanted the record executives to hear. One of the top executives cut him short saying, "Before we listen to any of this guy's tape, let's see his picture." In other words, it may now be image first, talent second. Music videos have changed the music business forever.

In the motion picture *Indecent Proposal* the character portrayed by actress Demi Moore was offered one million dollars to have sex with the character portrayed by handsome movie idol Robert Redford. This motion picture was considered to be a "woman's movie" and, most probably, many women were excited by the situation presented by the plot; after all, it was about romance. Let's assume that everything (photography, settings, actors, script) about *Indecent Proposal* remained the same except that Redford was replaced with an actor who was grossly overweight and bald. Would it have been the same story? Would it have had the same impact on women? We believe the Redford replacement would have removed the element of romance from this movie and completely changed its meaning and impact.

Today we are being bombarded with images on television, magazines, videos, and in the movie theaters. Never before in history has your image been such an important factor in gaining success.

MEN AND WOMEN: SURVIVAL OF THE FITTEST

The significance of image is ingrained in the very fabric of human nature. One of the prime reasons for the evolution and survival of humans is found in the reproductive process, where the strongest genes from both male and female combine to create even stronger offspring. There is within all of us a powerful drive to find a suitable mate. The biological laws of evolution dictate that if two human beings with above-average intellect or above-average physical prowess should mate, their superior (dominant) genes will produce superior children. The new technology of genetic engineering may someday improve on nature's gene selection process, but for today we are still the result of our parents' gene pool.

The dating-and-mating game is influenced by the natural instinct of both the man and the woman to mate with another human being of sound intelligence and good physical characteristics. This desire for sexual contact with physically and intellectually stimulating people does not diminish with age. One of the most important tracking devices used when looking for a mate is the eyes. Once again we're right back to the fact that we act as though "the way someone looks on the outside reflects the way they are on the inside."

This human quest for intimacy, or any connection with individuals we perceive to be superior, manifests itself in forms of hero worship toward athletes, entertainers, scholars, and successful people in general. The advertising industry knows that

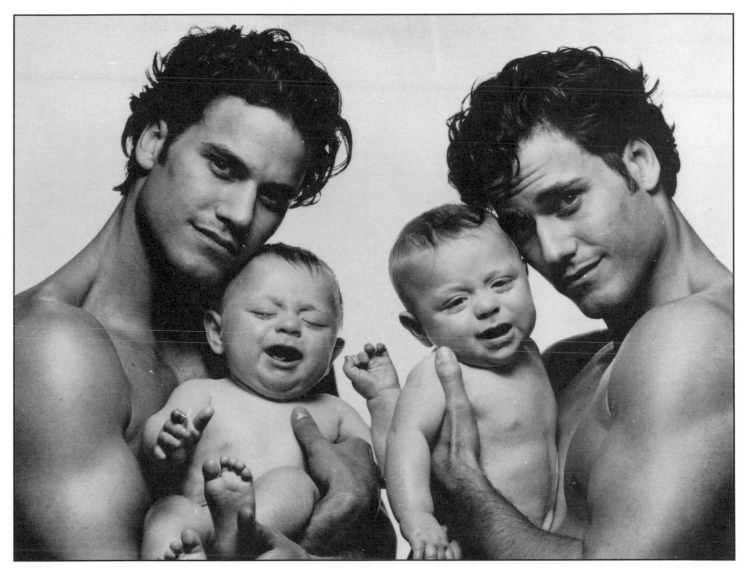

Survival of the fittest through Image Enhancement Technology. (Photograph courtesy of Michael and Walter Mocellin, and Barbizon Academy of Ontario, Canada)

the images these people convey to us are attractive and alluring, so much so that we seek to imitate them with respect to clothing, hairstyles, cologne, interior home decorating, our choice of an automobile, and the like. When you consider the importance of masculine image in areas such as politics, the media, the business world, and in your social life, a poor image may cause you to become a spectator rather than a player in the game of life.

6

Female Fantasy

Our company, Dorian Cosmetics, has been marketing makeup for men through mail order for more than eight years now. During this time we have encountered a type of customer who we never could have imagined when we started out. In virtually the very first month, we began to receive orders from women. At first we thought these women had misunderstood our advertisement, so we called them to verify that they were ordering makeup for men. The outcome of each telephone conversation was always the same: these women were ordering the makeup for the men in their lives. At first this profoundly surprised us, but as we can now see, women buying personal items for men and vice versa is a very important factor in contemporary consumer purchasing. An example of this in reverse is the fact that many of the customers at exotic lingerie shops, such as Frederick's of Hollywood, are men. They are purchasing silky items and revealing garments as gifts for the women in their lives. The real truth is that when their women wear the "gifts," the men get to live out one of their fantasies. We often buy such things as perfume, clothes, and jewelry so that women can help us realize our own personal fantasies. The sales of exotic undergarments, for both men and women, has increased dramatically during the past five years. This demonstrates that there is now an emphasis on all aspects of the physical human being, a phenomenon unparalleled in modern history.

Until relatively recently, women's fantasies were rarely considered important by the advertising industry. When advertising a new car in 1960, a few sexy female models standing around the vehicle seemed to be the mandatory formula. This type of advertising was directed at the man. The implication was that if he bought the car, somehow his sexual magnetism would be enhanced and he would gain the admiration of women and the envy and respect of other men. The majority of advertising that was directed toward women in 1960 was for home appliances, housecleaning products, or health and beauty aids. Since that time the earning power and the role of women in our society has evolved dramatically. Today's woman does not have or want the same lifestyle as her mother or grandmother, and her fantasies regarding a dream lover are much different.

We see an awareness on the part of contemporary advertisers regarding the powerful role women play in society. A significant amount of the advertising in the electronic and print media is now directed at women and their fantasies.

Men must realize that the average female also has strong sexual fantasies, which can be stimulated by such things as their sense of smell: hence this famous phrase from a well-known men's cologne advertisment: "The men in my life wear Brut or they wear nothing at all." The women of the nineties want their men to look good and even smell good. This is interesting when you consider that less than fifty years ago the men's fragrance industry did not even exist. The evolution of Western culture is shaping the modern woman's definition of her ideal man.

In the past, the phrase "sugar daddy" was used to describe an older, usually successful man who lavished gifts and money on some attractive young lady in return for her favors. Today there is a growing army of "sugar mamas": older women who seek the company of younger men. These women were raised in the value system of the 1940s and 1950s but they now feel entitled to act out their feelings and fantasies. Some of the most successful women in the entertainment world either live with or are married to younger men. In the past, for some reason, we thought it was all right when an older man married his child bride, but now many middle-aged men get upset when they see women their age seeking younger men. On the surface it would seem that we have a situation of the older woman wanting a young stud, but in most cases this is not necessarily true. What

Not all women consider physical appearance their primary criterion for judging men, but (whether they admit it or not) it is a significant factor. (Photograph courtesy of Sharon Barber)

older people find especially attractive in a younger companion is the exuberance and excitement usually associated with youth.

Today women are obtaining parity with men, not only in their careers but in all other aspects of their lives. Just like her male counterpart, even the most successful career woman has many romantic and sexual desires longing to be fulfilled.

In many parts of the world women are still sexually restrained by their culture: they are made to wear loose-fitting clothing and in some countries they are required to cover their bodies and their faces in public. The role of the female in these cultures is sexless, and her relationship with her husband is that of slave to master.

Reaching back in time, less than seventy years ago, most women in the United States were not truly in touch with their sexuality. Within a period of two decades, from 1910 to 1930, two technical advances entered the lives of mainstream Americans, radically altering the culture and the relationships between men and women.

The first of these technological advances was the automobile. Prior to the proliferation of affordable assembly line vehicles, many women had been isolated from the outside world. The men whom they had occasion to meet and marry were either friends of the family or neighbors, but the coming of the automobile provided the opportunity to explore new territories and meet new people. Over the years the automobile has played a major role in promoting new relationships. Most couples who are together today would probably not have met if it were not for the automobile.

The second major cause of cultural change was the motion picture. Just as with the automobile, films were able to transport their audiences to mysterious and enchanting places and introduce viewers to many types of people never before known to exist. In darkened theaters throughout the country, emotions were awakened in women, often for the first time.

The single most significant factor in this awakening was the ultimate male sex symbol of the 1920s, Rudolph Valentino. When Valentino appeared on the screen as the Sheik with his hard muscular physique, perfect eyebrows, and Hollywood makeup, his impact on women was incredible. The Valentino craze gave birth to the phenomenon of the fan club, the forerunner of today's groupies. The Sheik haircut, with pointed sideburns and square back, became the rage among men from all segments of society, and "The Sheik of Araby" became one of the most requested songs.

The word "chic" (pronounced like sheik) became synonymous with style and good looks. Valentino's picture could be found in all leading magazines and on the walls in the bedrooms of millions of women. Never before in history had any celebrity, whether a president or a sports figure, provoked this kind of female adoration. The presence of police for crowd control was required for all of Valentino's personal appearances. In 1926, at the pinnacle of his success, Rudolph Valentino died at the age of thirty-one, the victim of complications from a gallstone attack. When his death was announced, two women actually committed suicide outside the hospital; other suicides by female fans were reported around the country. His funeral was one of the largest in history. Women from all parts of the world came to pay their final respects to their dream lover. Until recently, fresh flowers were placed in front of Valentino's tomb on a regular basis by women who had probably only known him as a flickering image in their private world. Moving ahead in time we find a young man who seemed to be every woman's fantasy, despite his funny first name—Elvis.

What are the fantasies of the average female? Leading sexologists have written volumes on this subject, and they all share one common truth: the fantasies of the average woman are not the same as those shared by most men. The major difference is that women's fantasies do not deal almost exclusively with the physical act of sex. Some women find it very exciting to imagine having a sexual adventure with some men who are completely different from those they have known in their established circle of family and friends. These titillating thoughts could be called the "forbidden love syndrome."

A good example of this syndrome can be found in the history of Boston, Massachusetts. The New England states were founded and settled by the Puritans. In the early 1800s the population of Boston consisted mainly of white Anglo-

Saxon Protestants who controlled most of the businesses, the property, and wealth of their city. With the onset of the potato famine in Ireland, thousands of Irish immigrants came to America, where they settled in the Northeast with a very strong concentration migrating to Boston. Most of the young Irishmen lacked the breeding and manners of the men in the established community. They were known as brawlers and drunkards, and were considered a blight on the culture.

Despite the reputation of these men, many women with Puritan roots found young Irish lads very attractive. For some of these women it was only a sexual fling to be kept secret from their families and associates; later they would marry men who were socially "acceptable." For others, an affection developed that was so strong they married their Irish men despite family objections. Some women were disowned by their relatives and were cut off from any inheritance because of their disgrace. Over the years, in part due to intermarriage with women of Puritan roots, the Irish developed their own wealth and social power base. Although the Irish were never fully accepted as equals by the original founding families of New England, they learned to coexist and became part of the established power structure of the region.

No matter what their social and economic position, most men are concerned about being "one of the boys" and blending in with their buddies or business associates. Women are very different in this respect; even though they may dress in a specific style, each wants to be noticed as an individual. It is most probably for this reason that a woman will become very upset if another woman enters a room wearing the same dress or outfit. Most women want to be individuals, and they admire individualism in men.

Women see through the male need for peer approval, and although some accept it as normal, others feel compelled to make the break and find a man who offers something different in the way of lifestyle, values, and physical appearance. Today this female attraction to men who are different crosses all ethnic and racial boundaries.

We all want the good things in life: a sharp car, a nice house, attractive clothes, and so on. These are our possessions, and judgments are often made about people based on the perceived value and style of their possessions. Whether men admit it or not, they often want a beautiful woman by their side because an attractive woman makes them feel better about themselves and tends to enhance their image. Is it therefore reasonable for men to believe that women also want attractive men? Isn't it also reasonable for men to believe that if a physically attractive woman can be more sexually stimulating for a man, then a physically attractive man would have this same or a similar effect on a woman?

Today, in our ever-changing workplace, a majority of single women are becoming financially independent. In increasing numbers they no longer require a male to provide for their security or to "put bread on the table" and, as we have discussed, the passion for "nice things" is not a masculine or feminine trait, but a human trait. When a woman selects the man she wants, that selection must add something positive to her life. We do not mean to infer that all women consider physical appearance to be their exclusive basis for judging men, but (whether they admit it or not) it is a significant factor.

We conclude this section with a very important truth. While men often define a "sexy woman" by her body parts (e.g., legs, breasts, and buttocks), women are not so fixated on specific parts of male anatomy; they are much more universal in their view of what constitutes a sexy man. Women are attracted to the *total image package.*

Contrary to locker-room tales (and this might prove to be a major disappointment to many men), the size of your penis is usually not the major factor in female fantasies. Concern over penis size is second only to impotence as the reason men seek sexual counseling at the Kinsey Institute. In a recent survey, both men and women were asked what they thought was the average size of an erect penis. The average response from women was four inches; the average response from men was ten inches. Statistics compiled by condom manufacturers indicate that 80 percent of males (African American, Caucasian, and Asian) have an average erected penis size ranging between four and seven inches. If you are below this average range, there is always the surgical enlargement procedure known as phalloplasty.

Approximately one-fourth to one-third of a man's penis size remains imbedded within the body; phalloplasty surgically exposes this hidden portion. The second phase of phalloplasty is to increase the circumference (thickness) of the penis by adding fat extracted from another part of the body. For those men who are extremely overweight, a loss of fifty to sixty pounds could bring back another full inch or more of penis size, since excess fatty tissue can surround the base of the penis and actually reduce its perceived size.

The reason most men would consider surgery is probably based more on personal levels of self-esteem rather than sexual performance. There are men with small penises who may be rated by women as terrific lovers because these men have developed a sophisticated understanding of the total sex act, including ejaculatory control and the exploration of their partners' sexual fantasies. In this enlightened world there are still many people who lack accurate sex education. Information that can help you and your partner to better sex is available in any number of places. For example, the Better Sex Video series offered by the Chapel Hill Institute for Sexual Enrichment provides explicit videotapes prepared by renowned psychologists, sex educators, and physicians covering the exploration, sharing, and acting out of sexual fantasies, as well as the video "You Can Last Longer," which offers solutions for premature ejaculation.

Despite the medical concerns over illness related to breast implants, talk show episodes and printed stories abound of women who have had breast enlargements to emphasize their figures and improve their sex lives. But gentlemen, the male counterpart is not true: if you could have your penis enlarged, let's say four inches, it probably would not change your social life one bit or make more women attracted to you. For the majority of women it's not the size of the wand, it's the magic in the magician.

YOUR IMAGE AND YOUR RELATIONSHIPS

Very often when talking to someone about the qualities sought in a partner, they will include the phrase "looks don't count." Men and woman alike will go on to say that the really important attributes in the person they are seeking are intelligence, personality, a sense of humor, and the like. There is, of course, no disputing the fact that these qualities are very important, but the reality is that one of the most important factors remains physical appearance. In order to get to know that special person of your dreams, you have to meet first, and there can be no denying that many romantic relationships begin with a mutual physical attraction. There is an old European expression: "The eyes are the scouts for the heart."

One subtle change that has occurred, especially within this past decade, is that women are now finally admitting that they are attracted to a man's physical body. Back in the 1950s, no woman would turn to her girlfriend and say, "That guy has nice buns." Nor would any woman ever dream of spending a night stuffing dollar bills in the G-string of some male dancer.

Although many men maintain a perfect lawn in front of their house and wash and polish their car every week, their own personal image is rarely a consideration. To us it seems strange and illogical that any man would be so meticulous in maintaining his possessions but give little thought to his personal image. On a Saturday afternoon he will spend hours detailing his car, yet all the while his belly hangs over his belt.

One of the components of a truly happy life is a successful personal relationship. To some extent, relationships can be compared to a business partnership. In order to make it successful, both partners must constantly work at it. When both make a conscious and concerted effort to maintain and improve their appearance it can serve as a great source of stimulation within the relationship. If only one partner recognizes the importance of personal image, it could put a strain on the relationship.

Anyone with a basic knowledge of human nature knows that when people feel good about themselves they are much better partners. Many women spend a significant portion of their time stroking what they perceive to be a very fragile male ego. The fact is, feeling good about yourself cannot come from another person. Instead we hope to show you that it comes from within. To have a complete and satisfying relationship, it is essential that you feel good about yourself. Remember that great song "I've Got to Be Me," which was performed by Sammy Davis, Jr., in the Broadway play *Golden Boy.* In it we are told "I can't be right for somebody else if I'm not right for me." You are the artist of your image and the author of your destiny.

7

Clothes in on Your Image

Presenting an attractive masculine image has always been the objective in the design of men's fashion. Robes, cloaks, capes, and countless other clothing items provided the costume that immortalized many historical figures. In centuries past the clothing men wore served many purposes in terms of establishing their image. Much like the men of today, men in the past used garments to transform their physique to meet the desired styles of the period. In the Middle Ages it was not uncommon for a man to pad his shoulders, chest, and buttocks creating the then fashionable "S" look, when viewed from the side. Some men would also stuff the calf area of their hose to give the lower leg a more muscular stance. After the introduction of men's hosiery (not altogether unlike the tights of a male ballet dancer) came the bold projecting "codpiece," which was worn over the genitals. These codpieces were colorfully decorated and stuffed upright to suggest virility. By the mid-eighteenth century, men were presenting the natural shape of their bodies as fashion was influenced by the classical statuary of Greece and Italy.

Now, more than at any time in history, men are spending more time in the gym sculpting their bodies. The average shoulder width has increased and the average waist line has decreased. Evidence of this can be found in the male modeling industry, where the preferred jacket size is now 40 or 42 regular when only a decade ago it was 38 to 40 regular. These changes in men's fashion are closely monitored by the Fashion Association. The membership of this trend-watching organization includes some of the finest designers of men's clothing creating suits with wider shoulders, fuller arms and legs, but slimmer waistlines.

Today the peferred fashion look is stylishly casual, but the formality of a black tie affair still requires a tuxedo. The accessories you chose also play a very important role. It is important that you learn how to tie your own bow tie: this makes it clear that you are not a "clip on" guy.

Yesterday conformity was virtually a prerequisite for success in the corporate world. In the new global economy corporate America is going through a "downsizing" of its support staff at all levels. Literally millions of executive, management, and white-collar jobs have been eliminated, with new announcements of layoffs occurring with alarming frequency. The old requirement to conform may no longer always be an asset. In this new age of individual enterprise, rigid conformity may even be a liability for those who may find it advantageous to stand out among the crowd. It is often said that most of the men who were responsible for starting great corporations could never have worked for the very corporation they created, because of their independent spirit and fierce individuality.

During the early 1990s, corporate giant IBM experienced a tremendous decline in profits and was forced to lay off thousands of employees worldwide. One financial analyst was quoted as saying, "IBM stopped being innovative in the marketplace." IBM always had one of the most conservative dress codes in the corporate world: it may be that mandates for a conservative image in large corporations may have generated narrow conservative thinking, which often runs counter to innovation. Leaders of authoritarian countries such as China know that one of the ways to suppress individuality, independent thought, and creative enterprise is to make everyone dress and look the same. Many major corporations are now realizing that a mistake could have been made; a button-down shirt may promote a button-down mind. These same corporations are now attempting to encourage innovation by promoting "dress down days" in which employees are permitted to wear more relaxed attire. Ironically, we were recently told by an acquaintance that he forgot about dress down day at work and received glares and comments from coworkers. Let's hope that "dress down" does not become just another uniform.

There was a period between the mid-1960s and the mid-1970s when a great many men broke with tradition and let their hair and sideburns grow. They wore brightly colored shirts, wide belts, bell-bottom pants, and lots of jewelry. This relatively short-lived fad ultimately proved to be only another manifestation of male conformity. Many men are hyper, if not downright paranoid, about making sure they appear masculine. Here is just one illustration: the now popular pierced ear look only became a widespread phenomena after sports personalities and entertainers appeared on television wearing them. With that kind of legitimacy, more men began imitating the look.

We do not wish to imply that your personal image should exceed the boundaries of reasonable standards. Our point is that men are no longer chained to the extremely rigid dress and image restrictions imposed by the old corporate standards of the past, and breaking these chains could be an advantage for certain individuals.

When you go to your favorite bookstore you will no doubt find many "dress for success" books, most of which are based on the assumption that you are seeking to start or advance your career within the structure of a large corporation or in some other traditional environment. As previously stated, we do not recommend or endorse any particular image as being the ideal; however, there are some basic truths to keep in mind when it comes to the selection of a man's wardrobe, and these may be especially pertinent when choosing traditional attire. Though society is changing, the fact remains that many of the men and women who possess the power to have a positive effect on your life still relate strongly to traditional attire. A moderate style of dress indicates that you are a conforming team player. There is an old show business axiom that could serve as a general rule when dressing for success: "Package your appearance to fit your audience."

With the exception of your face and your general physical appearance, your clothes are the first thing that people see. How you dress can significantly influence the first impression people come to have about who you are. You may have invested

Left: Shirt and tie by Mondo di Marco Accessories (Mondo, Inc.). *Center*: Sportcoat and trousers by Cesarani (The 500 Fashion Group). *Right*: Suit by Principe of Marzotto. (Photographs courtesy of The Fashion Association)

Left: Double-breasted suit by Enrico Silvanni (Photograph courtesy of The Fashion Association). *Center:* Photograph courtesy of Michael and Walter Mocellin, and Barbizon Academy of Ontario, Canada. *Right:* Photograph courtesy of Sharon Barber.

in various external image-enhancing possessions such as a gun collection, a beautiful home or apartment, art, fine furniture, and the like, but you cannot bring these things with you when you venture out of the house to make a living or to a social occasion. One of the best image investments you can make is the money you spend on your wardrobe. It is one of your most significant image symbols.

Styles change. Any one who has seen photographs dating from the 1800s through the 1940s knows that a hat was always standard apparel for the well-dressed man. As recently as the early 1960s, many major organizations continued to insist that their marketing and sales people wear a hat when calling on clients. However, with the trend toward longer hair for men, the wearing of hats decreased markedly and the industry shrank. This period signaled the end of an era in men's fashion. If being contemporary is important to you, keep abreast of men's fashion magazines and choose clothes from the most current styles that flatter your physique, highlight your personal tastes, and fit your budget.

Regardless of your career path or the image you may wish to portray, never be without at least two quality suits for those occasions when a suit is mandatory. All clothing can be placed into three broad categories: conservative, traditional, and fads. Unless you are in a fast-track, highly visible profession such as promotion, advertising, or entertainment, or you just happen to have a lot of money to spend, you should avoid fads. As their name implies, they come in and out of style much too fast. Years ago a friend of ours bought a fad item called a Nehru jacket. He was able to wear it for only two weekends then it was out of style. Oddly enough, if he still had the jacket today—and he could fit into it—he could probably wear it again since the look seems to be on the way back.

The most important business consideration in purchasing your style of suit depends upon your customers, clients, or associates. In other words, who are the people who can influence your life, and how might your selection of clothing influence them? Since a suit is such a powerful image statement, it should always reflect style and quality. Oftentimes, when you purchase an inexpensive suit of poor quality, you are discounting your image. For today's smart buyer there are many men's clothing factory outlet stores throughout the country, where you can find real quality at reasonable prices.

When buying a suit, make sure it fits you and you fit it. Always look at the fabric label: for example, worsted wool and wool or silk blends usually indicate quality; polyester or linen, which tend to lose their shape, are usually not recommended. Never be influenced by a salesman or tailor into extensive alterations: a reputable clothier knows that the line and balance of a suit can be altered only slightly, measuring in quarter inches. Try on the suit and stand in front of a triplex mirror at normal posture, look at yourself from all sides. How do you look? Now fill your pockets with items you normally carry such as wallet, glasses, and car keys, then walk around, sit down, cross yur legs, and fold your arms. Does the suit feel comfortable?

Your choice of shirts, ties, shoes, or underwear are strictly a personal choice. For information on the latest styles we suggest you subscribe to any number of quality fashion magazines such as *Gentleman's Quarterly* (*GQ*), *Details*, *Esquire*, or *Playboy*. We also suggest a subscription to the excellent catalog offered by *International Male*, where you will find an exclusive line of shirts, trousers, and sportswear, not available through traditional retail sources. These publications can be found on any well-stocked newsstand.

To say that image is the key to financial success would be ridiculous, but to say that image is *not* important in obtaining that success would be even more absurd. Prior to the making of the movie *Wall Street*, image consultants were called in to develop Michael Douglas's on-screen image. The hairstyle, suit, and tie combined to produce what is known as "the power look."

More now than at any time in history, a man's image may determine the extent of his business and social success. Within the next few years, the technology of interactive multimedia will radically effect our lives and our culture. For example: we will be doing a great deal of our shopping from home by utilizing interactive television technology. Many of us will not have to leave the house to go to work since our new workplace will be in front of a computer monitor. Although we may never have to leave home for work in this new world, one element of career advancement will probably remain the same, the traditional job interview. Technology will provide to perspective employers the ability to verify instantaneously all references of a prospective employee: university transcripts, prior job performance, and whatever else would qualify you as a strong candidate for an open position. The technology of video conferencing may someday make it possible for you to interview for a job while seated in your living room, but however distant the process becomes, the fact remains that employers still want to *see what you look like.*

Even though every aspect of your resume matches the requirements for the job opening, perspective employers will want to *see you.* A job interview can be a very important event; getting the job you really want could change your life. The good part about most job interviews is that advance notice is usually given and there is time to prepare. Before you are evaluated by an interviewer, evaluate yourself in front of your mirror. Keep in mind that one intangible requirement of many positions is that your image match the look the company desires for the specific position. Before any interview, do a little research on the company to determine as best you can the image profile of its personnel.

Looking back, most people can recall an unplanned evening or impromptu event that changed the course of their life. Many opportunities that present themselves arise without any notice so we must be ready to seize the moment and "be prepared" because any moment could be the chance of a lifetime. Your image could determine if you will ever get that chance. How many opportunities have you already missed, and how many more were there that you were never aware of? Every day ordinary situations hold the promise for "that most important interview." Always be prepared, bring your best image with you or, as the commercial for an international credit card company concludes, "don't leave home without it."

Have you noticed that most successful men *look* successful? But which came first, the look or the success? Do these men look that way because they are successful, or are they successful because of the way they look? To dress *as* a success is a much more powerful statement than dressing *for* success.

8

Your Height: What Are You Up To?

The motion picture business has always depended on its ability to create images for stars, both on-screen and off. Back in the 1940s, one of the leading men in Hollywood was Alan Ladd. He was handsome and a very good actor, but he was rather short—often shorter than some of his leading ladies. According to Hollywood legend, several different devices were used to compensate for this problem. When Ladd stood next to his leading lady on screen the scenes were generally shot from the waist up because he often had to stand on a raised platform, or the leading lady was positioned in a ditch to do the scene, because the producers knew women generally prefer tall men. We have often heard women describe their dream man as "tall, dark, and handsome." The exception to this might be Southern California, where the description probably is "tall, blonde, and handsome." No matter, the first requirement is tall. The emphasis on height should not be surprising: when describing another person, one of the first things we usually mention is height.

Medical technology is currently involved with intense research in the area of growth hormone therapy in the hope that one day each person's ideal height will be predetermined before birth. Unfortunately, none of us have had the benefit of this technology. Thus far none of us have had any control over how tall we became: height is just part of the genetic crap shoot, with our parents' genes rolling the dice. You may not have any control over how tall you *are*, but by using Image Enhancement Technology you can control *how tall you appear*.

Why Would You Want to Be Taller?

Your height is part of your total image. If you are six feet, six inches or four feet, six inches, either of these extremes may well become the predominant factor in your image. According to current U.S. military statistics, the current average range of a new recruit's height is between five feet, nine inches and six feet.

Because of improved technologies in farming and food processing, and our ability to transport fresh foods to market, the nutritional quality of our food has been significantly upgraded. During the past century, improvements have added about four inches to the height of the average man. The average height for a soldier in the Union Army during the Civil War was five feet, six inches, whereas the average height of a male soldier in today's army is about five feet, ten inches.

Studies have shown that there may be a direct correlation between how tall a person is and how much money that person earns. We are all caught up in thinking that "bigger is better." The mark of success in today's career is often a bigger house, a bigger boat, or a bigger swimming pool. The fact is that the bigger man often gets the bigger paycheck. Here are some facts regarding the relationship between height and earnings.

- Many police organizations have a minimum height requirement that automatically excludes millions of shorter men from law enforcement occupations paying above-average wages.

- Virtually all presidential elections held since 1900 have been won by the taller candidate: Former President Ronald Reagan is six feet, one inch; George Bush is six feet, two inches. One of the Republican election slogans in 1984 was "Back Standing Tall."

- The following is a report, compiled by Ralph Keys and printed in *Esquire* magazine in November 1979. It shows the relationship between height and earnings during the year 1978.

SALARIES AND HEIGHTS OF U.S. ARMY CADETS

Height	1978 Mean Salary
5'3"–5'5"	$14,750
5'6"–5'7"	$16,500
5'8"–5'9"	$17,000
5'10"–5'11"	$17,500
6'0"–6'1"	$19,000
6'2"–6'3"	$18,500
6'4"–6'6"	$19,500

If this fifteen-year-old survey shows increased earnings for taller men within a U.S. government agency, imagine what the impact of height must be in today's image-conscious corporations. It has been said that every inch over five feet seven inches" is worth additional earnings in the corporate world.

Women will often say "I want a man I can look up to." This is meant both literally and figuratively. A woman wants a successful man with sound intellect, but she also wants to look up into his eyes when on the dance floor. Humankind has evolved to its present position on earth by mental superiority over the other creatures, but for centuries many tribal leaders were selected because of their physical strength. Size is frequently viewed as an indication of strength. Somewhere buried in our subconscious may be the idea that size is the indication of a leader, or an indication of superior sexual power.

If you are below average in height, or would just like to appear a little taller, there are a few things you can do to give yourself the visual perception of added inches.

- Wear clothes that give you something designers call a "long line." For example, if you want to look taller, *do not* wear baggy shirts or trousers; instead wear more form-fitting clothes. Anything that makes you look wider will make you look shorter.

- Pay close attention to the design on your shirts: horizontal patterns make you look shorter while vertical patterns make you look taller.

- Choose your hairstyle and hair color carefully. Since the top of your head is as far up as you can go, do not draw attention to yourself by some exotic hairstyle.

- If you are at all overweight, bring your weight into normal range. A bulging waistline could actually make you appear shorter. The leaner you are the taller you look. Recently we heard about a wiry friend of ours being described as "long and lean" although he is only five feet, nine inches tall.

These hints could help you look taller for those special times such as job interviews or when people see you walk into a room even from a short distance. But how can you influence the way your height is perceived when someone is standing next to you? *Image Enhancement Technology can now actually make you taller.* If you are five feet, seven inches you can become five feet ten inches. If you are already 5 feet 10 inches, you can become 6 feet 1 inch. *Image Enhancement Technology can increase your height up to three inches immediately.* The technology involved in the current design and manufacture of elevator shoes now gives you an undetectable solution to compensate for the shortcomings of nature.

The Richlee Shoe Company, located in Frederick, Maryland, is one of the world's largest manufacturers and distributors of elevator (Elevators®) shoes. Its catalog features fashionable shoes of every conceivable style ranging from loafers to wing tip and from western boots to sport shoes and sneakers. Your coauthors are both about five feet eleven inches tall but have worn elevator shoes for years. When leaving the house, we are between two and three inches taller, depending on the style of shoe we wear.

Unlike the past, today's shoe manufacturers can provide both height enhancement and style. (Photographs courtesy of the Richlee Shoe Company)

Why would anyone who is five feet, eleven inches wear elevator shoes? We wear them because *being taller is an advantage* and we always try to give ourselves every advantage over the competition, in any situation we may find ourselves.

The technology of the Richlee Elevators® utilizes a special construction that makes it look exactly like a regular shoe. This construction permits the use of an "inner mold" concealed inside the shoe, which cannot be visually detected by the casual observer. We have found the styling, quality, and workmanship of elevator shoes to be superior to many of the various brand name, conventional shoes.

Based on information regarding the image impact generated by your height, utilizing the Image Enhancement Technology offered by elevator shoes can raise your Image Quotient at least 1 point.

9

Molding Your Body

YOUR WEIGHT

The federal government has finally enacted a law making it illegal to discriminate against overweight people. To be overweight in today's world carries with it a social stigma. The prevailing theory is that obesity is a self-induced condition. It is believed that all overweight people are lazy, lack self-control, and have eaten themselves into their current physical state. For some people, their weight problems are of their own making, but for others the weight they carry around is in many respects a feature of their genetic makeup.

As a result of genetics some men are tall while others are short, some have a great head of hair while others are bald, some are athletically inclined while others are not, and some are brilliant while others possess less intellect. Although personal lifestyle can play a large part in obesity, if sheer gluttony is excluded, the determination of whether you will be thin or fat can be found in your inherited genes. Have you ever seen a woman with a small torso (back, arms, waist, etc.) but then she balloons out with big buttocks and big legs? This is not from overeating: it is genetic. If it were overeating, her waist would also be large. Many men with soft, overweight bodies are a product of (untransformed) genetics. We personally know men who have "lucky genes." They live on junk food and still look great. We also know others who eat sparingly yet still have a mushy waistline to show for their efforts. All too often obese people are plagued by depression, which causes them to overeat, which deepens the depression and the vicious cycle continues.

When it comes to the subject of body fat, men have a definite advantage over women: women are physiologically designed to bear children, so their bodies contain more fatty tissue so they can store food for their offspring. Similarly, men who are genetically predisposed to be overweight have more round fat cells than their thinner counterparts. If your genetic makeup seems to have given you more of these round cells than you would like, don't despair; you can be thin, lean, and muscular.

For men, being thin doesn't mean being skinny. "Skinny" denotes weakness. "Thin" means becoming more lean and muscular. Your image depends in large measure on obtaining and maintaining the ideal bodyweight for your height.

If your overweight condition is genetic, is there anything you can do? We are very fortunate indeed to be living in this age of discovery. As we have demonstrated, and will continue to show, most of the negative image problems that have plagued men since the beginning of time can now be corrected utilizing the benefits of Image Enhancement Technology: Short men can become taller. Bald men can have hair. Weak men can become strong. Unattractive men can become handsome. And overweight, flabby men can become lean and muscular.

About four years ago, Richard took a family vacation to the Thousand Islands, in upstate New York. A friend, named Steve, happened to live in that area. Richard had known Steve for several years: they first met as contestants in the 1982 Mr. New York State bodybuilding contest. Steve owned a health food store and his interest in health and fitness brought him into the sport of bodybuilding.

Since they were going to be staying close by, Richard suggested that Steve and his wife drive up to the Thousand Islands and have dinner with him and his family. Steve arrived in mid-afternoon and, since it was too early for dinner, they decided to spend a few hours by the hotel pool. When they reached the pool and removed their shirts, Richard was surprised to see how much weight Steve had gained since the last time they met. Steve was about thirty pounds heavier and had probably added about four inches to his waistline. Steve must have felt self-conscious because he quickly explained that he was naturally "heavy-set" and had to "diet like crazy" anytime he entered a contest. Anyone looking at him that afternoon would have never guessed he was ever a bodybuilder. When they competed against each other Richard noticed that Steve had very little muscularity, and his midsection always seemed a little mushy—that was when he was "in shape." Now Steve seemed to have ballooned. The old friends had a very enjoyable dinner, and Richard did not hear from Steve again for about four months.

One night in early November 1989, Steve called Richard to say that he was coming to Buffalo to take a shot at the bodybuilding title of Mr. Buffalo for men over thirty-five years of age. He asked Richard to meet him at the theater before the contest. While he always looked forward to seeing Steve again, based on the condition he was in the last time they met, Richard figured his friend was wasting his time. As Richard drove to the theater where the contest was being held he started to worry that Steve might look foolish. There was no way anyone his age could rebound from fat to fit in only a few months.

For those who still don't know it, Buffalo can get a bit snowy in the winter and the weather made Richard late for his scheduled meeting with Steve in the lobby of the theater. By the time Richard arrived, the contest had begun. The first category was the senior division for men over thirty-five. Richard just made it to his seat as the announcer called out the contestants to the stage so the judges could make side by side comparisons. There were about eight men in the "over thirty-five" division that evening. Each contestant was called on stage, Steve's name was announced, but he did not appear in the lineup of contestants. Richard assumed that the contest promoters told Steve that he could not appear, or he never made it to the theater, because of the weather.

After the group comparison was finished, each contestant was called out individually to do his posing routine. When the fourth competitor's name was called to the stage, the public address system announced Steve. How could this be? When the fourth competitor walked on stage, it was not Steve. This man was what is known in bodybuilding as "ripped"; he looked like a human anatomy chart. Richard had to sit up in his chair, lean forward, and squint before he finally realized contestant number four was in fact Steve. The word "transformation" seemed inadequate to describe Steve's improvement. "Metamorphosis" was a more apt term. Needless to say, Steve won the contest and the overall title of most muscular. After the contest, Richard had to ask: how did Steve achieve such a muscular shape? His answer was straight to the point: diet and exercise.

Body fat will accumulate when food consumption exceeds the requirements of your physical activity. Aerobic exercise is the best way to help equalize this intake-output deficit. Aerobic exercise is the performance of an activity that elevates your heart rate for a given period of time producing proven cardiovascular as well as weight loss benefits. It also allows you to burn calories at a rate higher than the rate at which you consume food.

Fortunately the running craze of the seventies and eighties is dying off. This fad began to decline after Jim Fixx, the author who wrote the best-selling running books, dropped dead of a heart attack while running. The die-hard runners may say that because of his family health history, Jim Fixx probably lived ten years longer than he normally would have as a result of his running. Maybe they are right, but maybe he could have lived another forty years if he had applied one other principle. Jim Fixx's theory about stimulating the cardiovascular system is absolutely correct, in our opinion, but he did not apply one key health factor— moderation. The same can be said about taking vitamins: because one pill is good for you, that does not mean ten pills are ten times better. For those of you who are now or were into running, when is the last time you heard the expression "breaking through the wall of pain"? Today, even the most avid runner is beginning to know when his body is being warned. Pain is the signal our bodies give us that something serious may be happening. Without the aid of pain your appendix could break and you would be dead in a few hours. If you cut yourself but do not feel the pain, you could bleed to death. Because of our Western Judeo-Christian culture, we tend to believe that anything worthwhile must come about through some form of suffering and pain. Pain tells your body that something is wrong; ignoring it is very unwise.

It is a fact that the health benefits provided by aerobic exercise, such as running, can add years to your life and make you look and feel significantly better. Personally we do not feel that outdoor running is the best form of aerobic exercise since it jars the body. The impact that occurs every time a running step is taken can adversely affect your feet, ankles, shins, knees, lower back, upper back, and neck. Along with potential trauma to the bones and joints, excessive running may cause internal problems such as the malfunction of vital organs.

THE MODERN HISTORY OF PHYSICAL TRANSFORMATION

Within each of our hearts is the desire to become a better person and to improve the quality of life. We share a natural striving for improvement. We want to gain knowledge that will help us understand how we as humans fit in this universe. We all want to be smarter, richer, healthier, more attractive. This desire for self-improvement has given birth to a billion-dollar industry. Today audiocassettes, videotapes, and books offer excellent self-help information on a vast array of subjects.

There is an unspoken desire within the hearts of most men to become "more of a man." This desire comes from the inborn knowledge that we have the ability to improve ourselves physically as well as intellectually. We have known for hundreds of years that we can improve on our natural attributes. About seventy-five years ago there were men who developed systems to make us stronger and our bodies look better. Many of these pioneers of physical transformation marketed their systems through mail order. Included among these were men such as Siegmund Breitbart, whose advertisements began with the question "Are You Ashamed of Your Body?"; Charles MacMahon, who asked "Is Your Buried Treasure, a Sunken

Chest?"; Lionel Strongfort, whose advertisements wondered "What Kind of Man Are You?"

These questions were designed to make men stop and think about the way they looked. Most of the information offered in the books and courses of that era involved basic principles of bodybuilding. These courses recommended body exercises such as push-ups and deep kneebends, while others recommended weight training with barbells and dumbbells, and performing standard exercises such as curls, presses, and squats.

Bernarr Macfadden: The Father of Transformation

Just about everyone today is "into" physical fitness; we are all trying to look and feel better. Enter almost any major park in any major city and the walkways abound with joggers in running shorts, and at the beaches throughout the land people display their bodies in revealing bikinis or thongs. It is interesting to note that if anyone appeared at a park or a beach dressed this way around the turn of the century, they would have been arrested immediately for indecent exposure. Our entire value system was different in 1910: William Howard Taft was president, and his 300-pound girth was the physical model of the successful man. These were the waning years of the Victorian era in which the prudish codes of modesty prevailed. The established medical community did not realize the importance of diet or exercise and actually condemned many of the things we normally associate with good health and fitness such as a high-fiber, low-fat diet.

Almost one hundred years ago a man named Bernarr Macfadden attempted to give the world some secrets of a successful image. Since his message was in conflict with the prevailing traditions and mores of the time, his teachings were greeted with disdain. The following is a brief profile of this "Father of Physical Transformation."

We include this section to illustrate our point regarding resistance to change in accepted traditions and beliefs. We hope you recognize the message and that this brief account will serve as a source of motivation and encouragement, urging you to grasp the tools of enhancement technology that are now available to make your life better.

Various parts of this book make extensive use of before and after photographs. These contrasting pictures are visual proof that you can transform yourself from fat to thin, from flabby to muscular, or from plain to attractive. Although they are now used routinely in a multitude of product advertisements, the use of before and after pictures actually began in 1893 when the idea was conceived and utilized by Bernarr Macfadden.

There seems to be a transformation theme in the life stories of many successful men. Bernarr Macfadden started life in very humble beginnings. The unique aspect of Macfadden's success was that he used his own transformation experience as an example for others. Macfadden was a pioneer, a trailblazer in showing people that they had the personal power to control the way they look and feel. He often used before and after pictures of his students as proof of the positive results of his teachings. Despite his tremendous impact on our lives today, it is very possible that you may have never heard of Bernarr Macfadden.

Bernarr Macfadden was born in Mill Spring, Missouri, on August 16, 1868. His father died when Bernarr was six years old, leaving young Bernarr and his ailing mother in abject poverty. A few years later, his mother died from a disease then called consumption but better known today as tuberculosis. Alone and homeless, young Bernarr was handed around to various relatives until he was ultimately placed on a "work farm." He was a weak and sickly child and had a hard time keeping up with the rest of the boys on the farm. One day a doctor came to give physical examinations. After Bernarr's physical he overheard the doctor say, "The records show his mother died of consumption. It looks like the kid has the same thing." That night, at the age of twelve, Bernarr packed his few meager belongings and ran away to start a new life.

His experiences on the road as a "professional hobo" changed his life. During his travels he had occasion to meet an American Indian who taught him about natural healing using herbs, deep breathing, exercise, and other techniques. In less than a year all symptoms of his "incurable disease" had disappeared. Not only was his illness cured but, because of the things he had learned, he was now becoming a healthy, strong, and muscular young man. While traveling through the Midwest on a freight train, Bernarr recalled that he had a cousin in McCune, Kansas. When he arrived in McCune, his cousin, Ed Thompson, gave him a job running a printing press for the local newspaper, which Thompson owned. The newspaper was called *The Brick.*

All Bernarr could think about was his physical transformation; he was obsessed with health and strength. He purchased a set of cast iron dumbbells and trained with them every day. Ed Thompson became concerned that young Bernarr was too engrossed in developing his body. In those days only circus people lifted weights. One day, when they were together in the press room, Thompson picked up a copy of their newspaper and said to Bernarr, "The printed word on this paper is stronger than any man's muscle. It can make or break a man's reputation, or even start a war." These words, combined with the wisdom he had learned from his Indian friend, would give direction to Macfadden's life, a life that would impact generations to come.

There were two newspapers in McCune, and the increased competition forced the *Brick* to end publication. The closing of the newspaper left sixteen-year-old Macfadden unemployed. Bernarr decided that his mission in life was to let more and more people know about the benefit of a fit body. His mission was easier to express than fulfill. At age sixteen he had no money and no job. In search of work he decided to go to St. Louis. He believed that once he had a job he could begin saving enough money to start his own business, which would be centered around physical transformation. Once in St. Louis, he held several jobs, among them a construction crew worker and a laborer for the railroad. During this period he continued to build his body at a small athletic facility. It was at this facility that he had occasion to meet George Baptiste, a prominent heavyweight wrestler. Baptiste showed Macfadden the art of wrestling and the transformed Bernarr went on to win the Midwest middleweight wrestling championship.

As a result of his wrestling fame, Bernarr came to meet Alexander Whitley, who had invented a weighted pulley device that would prove to be the forerunner of today's various exercise machines. Whitley's invention was one of the first pieces of exercise equipment that were not free weights. Whitley and Macfadden became partners in marketing this pulley device; they even set up shop in a booth at the St. Louis World's Fair.

After his success at the world's fair, Macfadden established a personal training business and was soon able to secure a small bank loan, which he used to start the publication of *Physical Culture*, the first major health, fitness, and bodybuilding magazine in the world. Most of the self-improvement information found in the pages of *Physical Culture* would today be considered basic knowledge or even common sense: walking in the fresh air, avoiding the excessive consumption of red meat, eating lots of fresh fruits and vegetables, and performing resistance-type exercise on a regular basis.

As the popularity of *Physical Culture* magazine grew, Macfadden began receiving letters and pictures from readers who had followed his advice and transformed their bodies. One of these early letters included two pictures showing a student's dramatic transformation. Macfadden immediately knew that these pictures, showing visual confirmation of the results of his methods, would serve as positive proof that anyone could improve their image. He began to ask all readers to submit any pictures of themselves showing their improvements. The first before and after pictures ever used in advertising now began appearing in the pages of *Physical Culture*. The "before and after" section of the magazine became very popular, boosting circulation by more than 1,000 percent. For the first time in history, thousands of people were transforming their lives by transforming their image. They were looking and feeling better.

Due to the success of the "before and after" concept, Macfadden decided to run a contest in the magazine and award a cash prize for the most dramatic improvement. He received letters and pictures from all over the world and the popularity of *Physical Culture* magazine soared. Reaching out to further increase recognition for his cause, and to promote his new woman's magazine, *Health and Beauty*, Macfadden promoted the first major bodybuilding/beauty contest in history. This contest would determine the world's best-built man and woman. The show should have been the springboard that launched the physical fitness movement into national prominence but, as we know, this was not to happen for another sixty years.

August 7, 1905, was the night Bernarr Macfadden presented his Mammoth Physical Culture Show at Madison Square Garden. This was truly the first major-league physique competition ever held. One of the features of Macfadden's show was the offer of a $1,000 first prize to the winner of the men's and women's competition. Although Macfadden was brilliant, he was quite naive when it came to judging public attitudes. He made a huge mistake believing that he could have women compete in his contest.

In the early 1900s, one of the strongest political action groups in the Northeast was known as the Prudery Movement. This group actually had its roots in the original Puritans, who believed the human body to be an instrument that could be used by Satan, and that only when they reached heaven with a bodiless existence would they be pure and know real happiness. It is important to remember that this was a time when all women wore ankle-length dresses and long sleeves, even during the summer months. The men of the time, not exempt from the strict code of dress, were made to wear tank-top type shirts at many public beaches. This Puritan attitude had permeated the cultural fabric of American life; it was no suprise that the followers of this movement were known as Prudes.

The leaders of the Prudes were very powerful and wealthy men who had far-reaching political influence. The president of the Prudery Movement in 1905 was Anthony Comstock. It was his mission in life to "lead the forces of purity and smut-hunting in America." Comstock was aware of Macfadden's publications showing pictures of men without shirts and women with their arms, legs, and backs exposed. Now these photographs from the pages of *Physical Culture* magazine were going to come to life on stage. Comstock had just used his influence to close a Broadway play by George Bernard Shaw for violating public morals; he even had some of the actors arrested. After attending Macfadden's Physical Culture Show, Comstock issued another public warrant for Macfadden's arrest. In the warrant he stated, "I regard this presentation as the very height of public impudence and impropriety." The morning after the triumph of his show Bernarr Macfadden was arrested in his office.

The prosecution presented evidence during the trial to prove that Macfadden was guilty of presenting a show that "was morally unacceptable to public standards." These exhibits included:

- a photograph of Macfadden not wearing the required tank top;

- photographs of the winners of the woman's physique competition (These "shocking" pictures showed the female contestants with both their arms and legs exposed for all to see);

- a statue of the Venus de Milo taken from Macfadden's office at the time of his arrest and used as evidence to illustrate his love of lewd and obscene art objects.

In today's liberated world this warped and fanatical attitude concerning the human body barely seems possible (the Muslim faith notwithstanding). Even at that time, Macfadden really did not take this legal action very seriously. He was, however, stunned when at the end of the trial he was found guilty.

As a direct result of his conviction, Macfadden immediately discontinued all activities associated with women's fitness and bodybuilding and he stopped publication of *Health and Beauty*. Although Macfadden lived on for more than a half century, he never again attempted to promote women's bodybuilding in the United States, although he did run some pictures of female athletes in *Physical Culture*. We believe this incident negatively affected the fitness movement for years to come, and may have encouraged most privately owned gyms to maintain a men-only policy. Those few women who were still involved in physical training were robbed of the opportunity to show the world the results of their efforts. Thankfully, today, the concept of the physically fit woman is both accepted and admired.

It is interesting to note that some historians consider that night in 1905 the predecessor of all beauty contests.

Despite the setback he suffered, Macfadden's views prevailed and the popularity of *Physical Culture* continued to grow. He published an *Encyclopedia of Health*, bringing together all the information he had acquired on physical transformation through diet, exercise, and natural health practices. For the next five years things progressed very well, then Macfadden made a written public statement that once again incited the Prudes.

In 1910 the venereal disease syphilis was destroying thousands of lives every year. In response to this health crisis, Macfadden published a warning, in the form of a magazine article titled "Wild Oats." The negative public response to this article was unbelievable, and all because readers were unwilling to acknowledge the existence of this sexually transmitted disease. Macfadden was charged with sending pornographic material through the United States mail. As a result of this charge, he was sentenced to two years in the state penitentiary. The jail sentence was overturned on appeal, but his business and the magazine were virtually ruined.

Macfadden knew that the attitudes in Europe were more realistic, so he traveled to England while his associates stayed in the United States and attempted to revive what was left of his publishing business.

Undaunted by his prior experiences, and knowing that attitudes in Europe were more progressive, Macfadden promoted the first Miss Britain Contest in 1910. The winner of this contest was nineteen-year-old Mary Williamson, a female athlete who had gained notoriety as a swimmer and high diver. Later, at age forty-eight, Bernarr Macfadden married Mary Williamson.

While in Great Britain, Macfadden managed to reinstate his credibility through a series of lecture tours. His marriage to the young Mary and the announcement

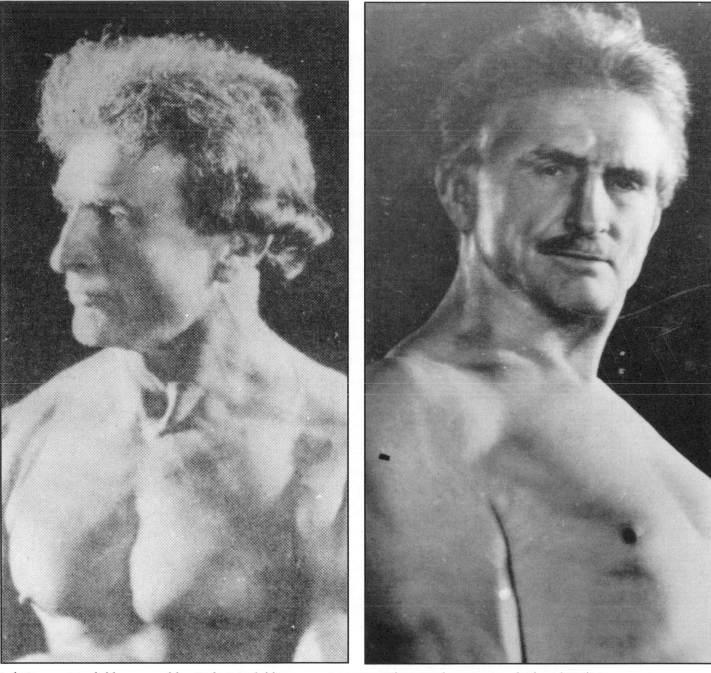

Left: Bernarr Macfadden at age fifty. *Right*: Macfadden at age sixty-nine. (Photographs courtesy of Edward Bodin)

of the birth of their first child received worldwide media attention. When Bernarr returned to the United States with his new bride and baby, he was warmly received. The public confidence in Macfadden and his teachings had been restored.

Although Bernarr Macfadden was now reaching his fiftieth birthday, his most successful years were ahead of him. During the next fifteen years he became one of the most successful magazine publishers in the world. Along with his first love, *Physical Culture* magazine, he was responsible for the publication of many of the nation's most popular magazines:

Liberty Weekly (circulation of 2 million weekly)

True Story magazine (circulation 2 million monthly)

True Detective (circulation 450,000 monthly) In this publication pictures and descriptions of the ten most wanted criminals were given to the public for the first time.

True Romances (circulation 675,000 monthly)

Photoplay (circulation 450,000 monthly)

Movie Mirror (circulation 300,000 monthly)

Radio Mirror (circulation 200,000 monthly)

Each year a total of approximately 13 million of Macfadden's magazines found their way into American homes, while another six million were translated and sold worldwide. Along with William Randolph Hearst, Bernarr Macfadden was one of the most successful publishers in the history of the industry. If Macfadden was so successful, why haven't we heard more about him?

Unfortunately, by the late 1930s poor business and personal decisions caused Macfadden's downfall. His publishing fortune, estimated at between $30 and $60 million in 1925, was gone along with his controlling interest in Macfadden Publishing. Although his great financial success and fame were behind him, Macfadden's spirit endured. At the age of seventy-four, divorced and virtually broke, he married a forty-two-year-old woman named Johnnie Lee. As a senior citizen, his youthful vitality amazed everyone.

To demonstrate the rewards and benefits of his teachings, he celebrated every birthday, after his eightieth, with a parachute jump. During his golden years Macfadden's sexual vitality, his indomitable spirit, and his love of life served as an inspiration to all men who thought the passions and pleasures of life end at age sixty.

Bernarr Macfadden died in 1955 after a lifetime of trying to spread the news that if you can accept change, it can transform your life; but change often means breaking away from some established traditions. Bernarr Macfadden was not infallible: some of his theories have been proven to be incorrect, but it is a fact that a great many of the things ingrained in our modern lifestyle were characterized a half-century ago as immoral or as the bizarre ravings of a "health nut." We, too, anticipate criticism. Evolving truth is often hard to accept when it is in conflict with established views.

THE TECHNOLOGY OF EXERCISE

Generally, when a man thinks of getting in shape or "working out" he pictures the unenviable task of lifting heavy weights countless times per day in the quest to develop the body of a Hercules. For all practical purposes this seems to be an impossibility for most of us. Who has the time or the desire to pump iron? If a choice has to be made, most men would probably rather increase their income by working extra hours than devote these same hours to getting into shape. But you don't have to face this choice. By engaging in proper exercise and diet you can strengthen, tone, trim down, and add muscle to your body without sacrificing your career, your family, or your social life.

The issue here is how much you really want to improve your image. Are you willing to do what it takes to keep yourself younger looking, healthy, and happy? If you're like most men, you'd answer with a qualified yes: the qualification being that you'd like to accomplish these things with a minimum investment of time and energy. Reaching and maintaining a healthy and fit body is not as easy as coloring your hair or adding inches to your height but with Image Enhancement Technology it is much easier today than it used to be.

Thanks to Image Enhancement Technology, we no longer have to risk the dangers of outdoor running to gain the health and image benefits of aerobic exercise. Many health and fitness experts agree that cross-country skiing is an excellent form of aerobic exercise. The smooth, nonjarring total-body motion of cross-country skiing provides a more complete body workout than some other forms of aerobic exercise such as walking, running, or cycling. It allows you to elevate your heart rate to a fitness-building level. By working both your upper and lower body, cross country skiing allows you to burn a maximum number of calories: up to 1,100 per hour. According to research, it also helps to raise your metabolic rate, so even when you're not exercising, your body continues to burn more calories because muscle tissue is being toned and transformed. By burning fat and toning muscle, cross-country skiing helps you trim inches and firm up in as little as twenty minutes, three times a week.

NordicTrack is one of the companies that offers an excellent cross-country aerobic unit. We mention NordicTrack because it is one of the leaders in the aerobic fitness industry. The issues of dependability and performance become very important factors when making a decision about an investment in any fitness product. The design technology and sturdy construction of all NordicTrack products make them solid investments over time.

There are other advantages of in-home cross-country skiing compared to running in the outdoors.

(Photograph courtesy of NordicTrack)

- You maintain your privacy.

- There are no dogs or muggers to bother you.

- You will not slip on the ice or on a wet spot in the sidewalk or the road.

- There is no need to invest in expensive running shoes.

- There are no hidden objects to fall or trip over.

- There is no danger of catching pneumonia from snowy or rainy weather.

- You will not leave your keys locked in the car.

- You will look and feel so much better.

Medical science has shown that the natural aging process causes your body to lose muscle mass and gain fat as the years go by. With that knowledge you can take charge and influence your future. From a purely physical standpoint you can slow down or even appear to reverse the aging process. A strength-training, muscle-building program, practiced regularly and diligently, will help you feel better and look better, too. By embarking on such a program, you will not only halt the loss of muscle mass but recapture it and build it up.

Along with adding muscle tone to your body, which helps you to better hold your shape and makes you appear more youthful and virile, a muscle-building program will also speed up your body's fat-burning capacity, something from which every man can benefit. Developing muscle burns additional calories at rest, more than any other tissue of the body. By adding muscle you will stoke your "fat-burning furnace," allowing you to stay lean.

When you consider the multiple benefits that better muscle tone and improved fat consumption can provide, a program to mold your body can be your ticket to a better looking you. Utilizing today's knowledge of exercise and nutrition you can achieve your body-image goals with a minimum investment of time and energy.

Although technology has rendered obsolete the traditional male role in our culture, and the need for muscle power is shrinking by the second, the emphasis and importance of a man's muscular physical image has increased. Fit and trim have become important components in contemporary society.

Years ago the layout of most gyms and health clubs consisted of racks of dumbbells, barbells, benches, and maybe a pulley apparatus known as the "lat" machine. Prior to the early 1970s, men who wanted to develop their bodies had to work with free weights. Men who chose to develop their muscles or increase their strength used free weights, but some individuals encountered problems, most particularly injuries caused by not using the correct form while lifting.

Around 1970, inventor Arthur Jones introduced a series of exercise machines he called Nautilus. Nautilus machines were constructed using a system of gears and pulleys connected to the weights. There was a Nautilus machine to develop each body part: a biceps machine, a triceps machine, and so on. Nautilus centers began to open all over the country. For many people, these machines offered advantages over free weights by providing the maximum angle of resistance, while minimizing risks of injury. The concept of machines replacing free weights as a method of strength training became very popular. Today we have reached the point where only one machine performing a multitude of functions is required to get a complete body workout.

NordicTrack has also spent a lot of research and development time to create a resistance training machine called NordicFlex Gold®. NordicTrack engineers took two years to study human anatomy, muscle physiology, physics, and biomechanics. The result of this study is a level of technology previously available only on the most expensive health club machines or on sophisticated rehabilitation equipment found in hospitals and clinics.

For the average man who trains at home, using an exercise machine such as NordicFlex Gold® offers numerous benefits over other exercise alternatives.

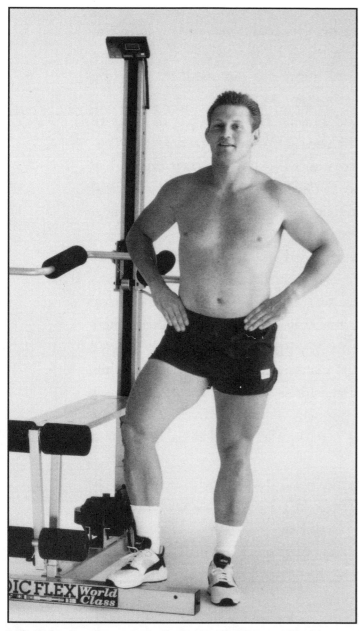

Left: Before working out with the NordicFlex Gold®, Don, age twenty-seven, had a body weight of 194 lbs., with 11.5% body fat. His waist was 33 inches, his arms were 12.5 inches, and his chest was 40.5 inches. *Right*: After using the NordicFlex Gold® for approximately three months, his body weight dropped to 175 lbs., with 6.0% body fat. His waist dropped to 31 inches, his arms increased to 15.5 inches, and his chest increased to 45.5 inches. (Photographs courtesy of NordicTrack)

Space: A single exercise machine takes up much less living space than a collection of free weights and benches.

Time: In the time it would take just to get in your car, drive to a gym, workout, and then return home, you could complete an entire recommended home workout.

Cost: The cost of an exercise machine is probably less than a two-year membership at most commercial gyms or health clubs. Money spent on a good-quality machine is a sound, long-term investment. Your dividends will come in the form of a stronger, healthier, better-looking body.

Availability: The equipment you may wish to use at a commercial gym is often being used by someone else at the time you need it. Your home exercise machine is always available.

Partial workouts: There are days when your schedule does not permit the time for a complete workout. Having a machine at home permits you to gain the benefit of an abbreviated session.

Safety: There are no heavy weights to drop on you. In addition the technology of the exercise machine adjusts to your own strength, never giving you more resistance than you can handle. The isokinetic resistance used in NordicFlex Gold®, was originally used by physical therapists for the safe rehabilitation of injured muscles.

To keep informed on the most current developments in the technology of exercise, subscriptions to magazines such as *Exercise for Men Only*, *Men's Exercise*, *Natural Bodybuilding*, or *Men's Health* would be helpful. The editorial policy of these magazines reflect a realistic, common sense approach to improving the health and well-being of men. The articles in these magazines are written for the man who wants to look and feel his best.

By utilizing today's knowledge of exercise and nutrition you can achieve your body-image goals. (Photograph courtesy of Michael and Walter Mocellin, and Barbizon Academy of Ontario, Canada)

THE TECHNOLOGY OF BIOCHEMISTRY

The Principle of Muscle Development

Have you ever shoveled dirt to make a fence post hole, turned over all the soil in your back yard, or performed any unusually strenuous activity? How did you feel the next day? If you're like most people you were stiff and sore for a while. If you ever observed highway construction crews or workers for utility companies, you would notice that many of them engage in strenuous physical labor for long periods of time. How can they do it without experiencing significant muscle pain?

Your body is an amazing thing: it makes adjustments to accommodate even such strenuous activity. This is the reason that the laborers involved in road construction do not get stiff or sore after a day's work. If you were to dig fence post holes every day, your body would strengthen to prepare you for this task. Soon you would no longer experience any soreness or discomfort. Something else would also happen: some of your muscles would become larger.

Many experts in the field of muscular development believe that nutrition is at least as important as exercise. If you ever look at issues of older muscle magazines from say 1955 or 1960, you will see that the physiques of the men pictured are no where near the quality of those seen in the magazines of today.

There are three reasons for this qualitative improvement:

(1) anabolic steroids,
(2) exercise technology,
(3) diet/supplementation technology.

Any rational man would totally reject the use of anabolic steroid drugs as a way to obtain a more muscular physique. The proven dangers of these drugs have been well documented. There are, however, safe and effective nondrug formulations that can significantly aid your progress toward obtaining a hard, muscular physique. These formulations have been developed as a result of both university and independent studies on the relationship between various nutritional substances and muscle growth.

Science has found that there are two physiological cycles at work in muscle tissue. The first is *anabolism* or the building phase of the muscle (hence the name *anabolic* for drugs that build muscle). The second cycle is called *catabolism*, when muscle tissue is depleted because it is in an energy-converting process. When you exercise you put a workload on your muscles. That workload causes the catabolic stage to activate. That "pumped" feeling you get after working out is not new muscle being formed; it is just a rush of blood that has been sent to a muscle group to help it perform the work you have placed upon it. If you were to measure your arm a few hours after a heavy workout, you might find that it is actually smaller than it was before you exercised; this is the result of catabolism. Your muscles do not grow during exercise: the growth occurs during the periods of rest that follow a workout.

The anabolic (muscle forming) activity in your body is highest between puberty and your mid-twenties. During these years anabolic activity begins to decrease and catabolic activity increases. This change in physiology is the reason men tend to lose muscle size and strength as they get older. Very often, old people are referred to as being feeble; this is because the function of anabolic activity that regenerates muscle fibers has been superseded by higher levels of catabolic activity.

Obviously, what you must do to build your body to its full potential is to maximize anabolic activity and minimize catabolic activity. Once again, the combined science of biochemistry and Image Enhancement Technology now provides every healthy man of any age with the ability to add lean muscle while loosing unwanted body fat. We repeat: exercise is a key factor in the development of muscular tissue, but diet is equally important. Just as in the case of hair growth and height, some men are genetically gifted with a tendency to be muscular and athletic. The Image Enhancement Technology of biochemistry offered by engineered foods, such as Dr. A. Scott Connelly's MET-Rx™, can now help transform the ordinary man to a level of physical excellence that would not have been obtainable in the past. MET-Rx™ contains a formula called Metamyosyn, a proprietary formula containing protein isolates. Each protein isolate is included in a precise amount based on its amino acid profile. Metamyosyn is combined with the precise combination of other nutrients in the MET-Rx™ formula; the effect of the ingredients of this formula is to work as a "partitioning agent," which is a combination of high-tech nutrients that are directed toward lean muscle tissue instead of fat, provided of course that you exercise regularly. The combination of a good diet, engineered food, and exercise will achieve results.

Diet and the Technology of Engineered Foods

Richard's story about Steve focused on bodybuilding but weight control through proper diet and exercise will work for everybody. We are convinced that diet contributes more than 50 percent to the success of any effective weight loss program. One of the most important factors in achieving weight loss is a reduction of fat in your diet.

There is a condition known as lacto intolerance, which renders some individuals unable to digest milk or any type of dairy products. People with this problem usually have their ancestral roots in the Middle East or in parts of Africa; those with roots in central Europe thrive on dairy products. There are some who find a vegetarian diet perfect while there are others who feel they cannot sustain a proper level of health and vitality without consuming some meat. For this reason we will not recommend a specific diet, but for your information the following is an example of the authors' typical diet.

Breakfast:

Bran cereal mixed with wheat germ, and skim milk
A cup of herb tea
Fruit such as cantaloupe, watermelon, or strawberries

Lunch:

Tuna fish sandwich made with diet wheat bread and mixed with non-fat mayonnaise and some green peppers
A glass of skimmed milk
A piece of fresh fruit

Dinner:

Broiled chicken (or turkey) breast
Baked potato or rice (hold the butter or sour cream)
Vegetable
A glass of skimmed milk

Food is not like alcohol or nicotine: you can fall off the wagon and still reach your goal. Occasionally you can even indulge yourself with a prime rib or lobster dinner followed by some gooey dessert. These indulgences can actually reward you for the progress you have made.

The National Cancer Institute is currently involved in a 20-million-dollar research project called "Designer Foods." The objective of this project is the identification of the chemical components of food that show anti-cancer activity. The final result of this project may be the development of a food compound combining the anti-cancer ingredients. "Engineered foods" is the term currently used to describe compounds containing specific ingredients for a specific purpose. The first U.S. government project with food engineering is already underway.

Even with a diet of good food many men do not have the ideal metabolism to loose fat and gain muscle. A. Scott Connelly, M.D., who received his medical training at Harvard Medical School's prestigious Massachusetts General Hospital, is presently involved in intensive research on nutrients that prevent obesity and help build muscle mass and strength. Although Dr. Connelly excels as a cardiac and critical-care specialist, he has spent many years and invested a great deal of money in the development of an engineered food called MET-Rx™. Dr. Connelly has concentrated his efforts on isolating the health-enhancing components of food which improve the body's ability to build muscle and lose fat. Unlike vitamin supplements, Dr. Connelly's engineered food contains an array of customized amino acids blends, sophisticated proteins, minerals, electrolytes, and vitamins which you could only obtain by consuming a very broad variety of fresh whole foods.

MET-Rx™ is used as a meal replacement but the technology found in MET-Rx™ is completely different from most of the current diet drinks, powders, and meal replacement systems on today's weight loss market. The exact proportion of nutrients has been arrived at through years of scientific research. It is "nutrient dense" and produces specific advantages well beyond weight loss. The primary and most noticeable benefit of MET-Rx™ (combined with the right exercise program) are the loss of body fat and the stimulation of the internal processes that increase lean muscle tissue.

Today men who are genetically predisposed to be overweight can transform their bodies using the technology of exercise, such as that offered by NordicTrack and the technology of engineered foods such as MET-Rx™. As the famous commercial for a butter replacement once stated, "sometimes it's good to fool mother nature."

Utilizing image enhancement diet and exercise technology can raise your Image Quotient 1 to 2 points.

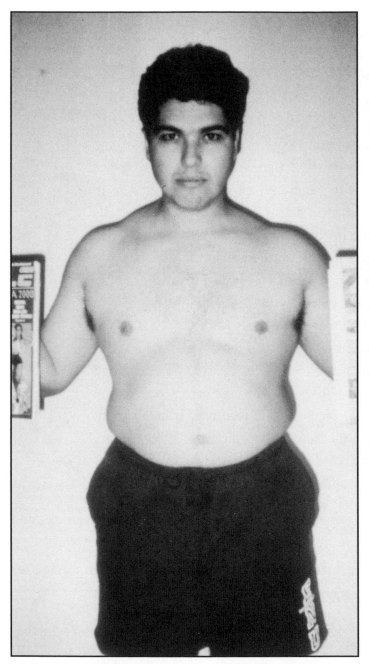 

Within eight to ten weeks, you can transform your image by utilizing the advantages of high-tech exercise and nutrition. (Photographs courtesy of Myosystems [MET-Rx™], Irving, Texas)

INVENT YOURSELF

Let's look at an ultimate image man of the 1990s—Arnold Schwarzenegger. His success story is well known to many. This son of a poor family in Austria set some very lofty goals at a very young age. He wanted to become the greatest bodybuilder in the world, and then be a star in Hollywood. These dreams proved to be more than childhood fantasies. Probably if teenage Arnold told anyone about his aspirations, they would have thought he was unrealistic and foolish. There was no way anyone could have known that he possessed three powerful attributes: desire, discipline, and an incredible knowledge of human nature. Schwarzenegger knew that it is an inherent part of human nature to admire physical strength and power. He also knew that in order to change his life he had to change his image.

He began his bodybuilding transformation at the age of fifteen. He never missed on his six-day-per-week workout schedule. He lifted weights in rooms so cold his hands froze to the bar. He tells interviewers that many times he lifted weights until he fainted or threw up. After six gruelling years of bodybuilding and a spartan diet, it was time for him to begin the quest for his goals. At the age of twenty-two he moved to California and, in a relatively short time, began to realize the fulfillment of his dream. During his years of competition, he won the Mr. Olympia contest seven times. The only obstacle left was his second objective, "to become a major Hollywood movie actor."

Although he starred in the movie *Pumping Iron* (a bodybuilding documentary), no one in the movie business considered him to have star potential. By 1992, Arnold was a number one box office attraction. He was ranked ahead of Mel Gibson, Tom Cruise, Harrison Ford, and even Jack Nicholson. Unlike many movie stars, Arnold Schwarzenegger never changed his name or employed some press agent to hide his background.

If you can find a bodybuilding magazine from the 1970s (1970–1975) with a picture of Arnold in it, compare it to a picture of today's "Terminator." You will note some image modifications. Where is that large mole that was on his left cheek? Why do his teeth look better? How could he appear better looking in 1995 than he did in 1973? Yes, even someone known as the world's most perfect man felt the need to become more perfect in order to get what he wanted. Arnold is very proud of the image he has crafted.

Arnold was not the first major personality to invent himself: to varying degrees most successful people from corporate executives and entertainers to politicians and media personalities are products of their own invention.

Our secrets of a successful image are not directed at men who are self-centered, egotistical, narcissistic, hedonistic, or materialistic. Instead, we direct our attention to the average man. Life is getting tougher; it is harder than ever to forge a successful career or develop meaningful relationships. All men need to understand and accept the truth about human nature as it relates to this new world of technology. The importance of education and knowledge cannot be overestimated, and the vital importance of your image can never be underestimated. At the beginning of each new year, many of us make resolutions to change things about ourselves and about our lives that we feel are in need of improvement—the dreaded New Year's resolutions. Many men have some notion of what they want to look like but have no real knowledge of how to accomplish their goal of looking better. We hope that this book helps you create a detailed blueprint for change so that you can transform yourself and become your own invention.

10

Your Skin

SKIN COLOR AND ITS EFFECT

In days gone by a man's wealth was determined by his girth and skin color as much as by his wardrobe and jewelry. Merchants, bankers, and royalty demonstrated their success in the form of soft, lily-white skin and a protruding belly. Pale, white skin testified that a man worked indoors rather than toiling in the fields. An expanded waistline was a sure sign that he was well off. Poor laborers who spent time in the fields earning a tough day's wages were characterized by dark tanned skin from constant exposure to the hot sun. They toiled day in and day out; their leathery faces and arms proved this beyond doubt. What's more, because of the long, hard labor and a lack of adequate food, these people were often thin and haggard.

In terms of desired appearance, the heavyset, pale man was the envy of those less well off. Even those who had little wealth would rather have been well dressed and elegantly plump, than wiry and dark. Pre-industrialized society frowned on the physical attributes of the working man, as much as on his lack of fine clothing or material possessions.

Today the roles are quite reversed. The Industrial Revolution sent the common laborer into the factories, where he slaved for hours on end to make a living. Wealthy men spent an increased amount of time participating in leisure activities, such as horseback riding, hunting, and other pastimes. Somewhere along the line the allure of a golden tan became more appealing, as did an athletic body. In the early twentieth century, sports activities began to gain popularity, as did the adoration of those who starred in them. Even before athletic competitions such as modern bodybuilding burst on the scene in the early 1960s, the public perception of what characterized a worthy man had significantly evolved. In the 1990s, a man who is fit, trim, and muscular, and who possesses bronze skin, is the epitome of success.

Think about it, what comes to mind when you see a man or woman who is very fair and/or a bit overweight? Pale skin cannot hide dark circles under the eyes or imperfections in the skin, in fact, a light complexion can make them more noticeable. Until recently only women and a minority of men in television and films have had the advantage of makeup. Seldom is a woman encountered who doesn't use some form of cosmetic coloring to enhance her appearance.

While skin cancer is not a condition any one desires, its threat does not keep people out of the sun. You need only take a trip to any beach on a bright summer's day to see all the sunbathers seeking a golden tan.

Truth be told, a tan does enhance the appearance of the skin, even as the causal factors (ultraviolet sun or tanning bed rays) damage and age it. As the skin pigment darkens to protect itself from further sun exposure it darkens in color, which can hide flaws while accenting other attributes. For example, a dark tan adds to the appearance of a muscular physique by bringing out the divisions between various muscles and body parts. Contemporary culture has already accepted the notion that characteristics such as wide shoulders, a thin waist, athletic legs, bulging arms, and a defined midsection are most noteworthy among men. Women look for such traits in prospective mates, just as much as men judge women for their physical attributes. Skin color can enhance the physical attributes we possess.

In terms of looking more attractive in today's world, the plump, white-skinned merchant of the 1800s is no longer the ideal. Like it or not, the public perception that a tanned, athletic body is the mark of a successful, desirable man will probably be with us for a while. All we can try to do is emulate this ideal. Even if a golden tan does put a finishing touch on this image, is it worth the effort or the risk?

Anyone who has been reading the newspaper for the past decade has been bombarded with information on the hazards of prolonged exposure to direct sunlight, especially today with the reported depletion of the ozone layer and the risks associated with exposure to ultraviolet rays. The danger is even greater for those whose ethnic background is based in Northern or Eastern Europe or the British Isles. For these individuals, their ancestors' physical characteristics evolved in a cooler, darker environment so they are even less equipped genetically to ward off the effects of prolonged exposure to the sun. A real problem exists by virtue of the fact that it is exactly these individuals who comprise the majority of men who feel that a deep tan is necessary to enhance their appearance. People of African, Asian, and Hispanic background face less risk but are not immune to any of the recognized skin problems caused by prolonged exposure to sunlight.

If you want to have the advantages of a golden tan without the risk, technology now gives you an option. Thanks to advances in dermatological science, safe, effective cream bronzers and sunless tanning compounds can be used to create a perfectly even suntan.

With today's technology there are now some outstanding sunless tanning lotions on the market. Unlike those of only a couple of years ago, the new preparations provide a very natural-looking, golden bronze tan. To some extent, these sunless tanning lotions can provide results far superior to the sun. Besides the obvious health advantage of not baking and aging your skin, they can be applied to achieve completely controlled even coverage. The technology found in today's sunless tanning products often generates results superior to a natural tan.

Our company, Dorian Cosmetics, offers a combination package called Tan Logic® consisting of a tube of body scrub and a tube of sunless tanning cream. We recommend the use of the scrub to rid the skin surface of dead cells. You may have seen some people who have used sunless tanning products and wound up with a blotchy, uneven, unnatural look. This problem is often caused by applying the cream in layers without removing the underlying dead skin. Using the scrub before applying the sunless tanning cream assures an even and completely natural-looking tan.

If you do go to the beach, or on any occasion when you will be exposed to the sun for a period of time, always use a sunscreen rated at spf 20 for minimum protection.

Your skin is medically classified as an organ; in fact, it is the largest organ of the body. It serves as a waterproof barrier that protects your internal organs from infection, injury, and the sun's harmful rays. Your skin is in a constant state of change since dead cells are being discarded and replaced by new cells from an underlying base. It is the result of this process that, over a period of time, you see changes in the quality and tone of your skin. Due to environmental and nutritional factors this often means an ongoing deterioration in both the skin's quality and texture. This is not necessarily a bad process, since by improving the quality of these new replacement cells through nutrition and care, you have the opportunity to improve your skin significantly. The quality of these new replacement cells is affected by both internal (nutritional) and external (environmental) factors.

INTERNAL SKIN CARE

The nutritional guidelines for meeting your skin-care requirements are basically the same as those for a healthy body, namely, the vitamins and minerals obtained from a balanced diet. There are, however, other vital elements that must be included to insure optimum activity of the sebaceous glands, which secrete oil that keeps the skin young and supple. World renowned Canadian physician Mark Vogal advises the separate daily intake of vitamins A and D in halibut-liver or cod-liver oil capsules. Dr. Vogal believes the oil not only provides required elements to the sebaceous glands, but also will lubricate your developing layers of skin from the inside out. When you consider that your skin is waterproof and designed to protect you from invasion by outside elements, moisturizing from the inside out is infinitely more effective than the application of any type of external moisturizing cream.

As we have said, one of the most important substances in your internal skin-care regime is water, the vital element that is sometimes referred to as the essence of life. It will improve and maintain your health, help you loose body fat and fight disease, and have a wondrous effect on our skin. There have been volumes written on the importance of water to every function of the body. One of the few things on which virtually every authority on health and fitness agrees is the benefits of drinking an adequate amount of water each day. The amount now often recommended is six to eight glasses of water daily.

EXTERNAL SKIN CARE

One of the major components in developing your physical image is exercise on a regular basis. When you exercise you perspire, which necessitates bathing or showering to remove the excreted waste products your body sweats off. Some dermatologists believe that people in the United States bathe and/or shower much too often, especially those individuals who are prone to dry skin. Frequent bathing washes away the essential oils that keep the skin flexible and youthful. Here are a few tips: When washing your face avoid excessively hot water; use a mild moisturizing soap; avoid using harsh cleansers and alcohol-based products (astringents), except when absolutely necessary. Both of these products will strip the skin of essential oils, resulting in a dry, flaky look.

WEIGHT CONTROL AND YOUR SKIN

There is nothing worse for your skin than rapid weight loss/gain, a phenomenon sometimes called the yo-yo effect. The dramatic expansion and contraction of skin tissue robs it of its natural elasticity, not unlike inflating and deflating a balloon too many times. For men who are just embarking on a fitness regime in the hope of filling out a thinner frame, take care not to gain your weight too fast. Rapid weight gain, even quick muscle gain, will cause stretch marks in the areas you are developing. If you are in the process of losing weight, do it slowly by combining the proper diet and exercise. Crash diets will leave your skin looking loose, you may also look older and drawn. The more serious drawback crash diets can have on your skin is that you usually gain back more weight than you lose and your skin begins the inflating/deflating cycle. Your goal should be to reach a weight you want and then keep it stable.

Utilizing the Image Enhancement Technology offered for internal and external skin care will raise your Image Quotient.

11

Your Hair: Using Your Head

SEEING IS BELIEVING

One of the newest and hottest terms in computer technology is "virtual reality," which consists of an audio-optical headset complete with two display screens that wrap around the eyes like aviator goggles, and earphones secured snugly by a head strap. This headset is connected to a computer capable of running special programs. The intent of virtual reality is to provide a complete immersion experience for its user. The program will make the user feel like a participant who is actually experiencing an event such as scuba diving, flying an airplane, or riding on a rollercoaster.

Because what is viewed seems so real the brain is tricked into triggering the physical sensations that often occur when the experience actually takes place. For example, virtual reality viewers will actually feel queasy during a simulated rollercoaster ride. The technology of virtual reality proves that our emotions and our senses can be altered and stimulated by what we see even if what we see is not actually taking place.

Some of you might ask: "What kind of person would make decisions based strictly on appearances?" The answer is, you do. To prove this point think back to your high school days. Remember that special girl all the guys had the crush on? We'll call her Debbie. She had blonde hair, blue eyes, and a great figure. She may have been head of the cheerleading team, class officer, a member of the most popular clubs, or maybe even prom queen. She looked like an angel who was out of reach for most of us, and, of course, she really was "a nice girl." Then there was another kind of girl in high school; let's call her Bertha. She was never a cheerleader and certainly never prom queen. She was overweight with bad skin and frizzy hair. You probably never think much about her.

Your judgments made on both of these young girls were based completely on physical image. Debbie became a cheerleader or prom queen because of the way she looked; and because of the way she looked, Bertha's high school days were filled with snide remarks and rejection. The impression given by Debbie is one of being interesting, exciting, and sexy. However, Bertha is not interesting; instead, she is viewed as dull and sexless. We have all known Debbies as well as Berthas, and the stereotypical description of either of them is not necessarily correct. There are some women who have been born a Bertha but have transformed themselves so that now the world sees them as a Debbie.

One of the tragedies for people who are judged negatively for the way they look is that sometimes their egos are so damaged that they will actually surrender their values and intellect and become what others have already judged them to be. The lives of many wonderful people, both male and female, have been ruined because of image problems they thought were impossible to correct. Fortunately today most men can significantly upgrade their image using Image Enhancement Technology.

Like clothes, hairstyles change regularly. Look at any movie that is more than five years old and you will see these changes. The hairstyles in some of the films from the 1960s and early 1970s actually appear comical by today's standards, but in another few years they may be right back in vogue. One problem with changing men's hairstyles is that certain ones—be they long or short, slicked back or wavy—look best on specific individuals, depending on the shape and structure of the person's face. Have you ever looked at an old photograph of yourself and thought, "Boy, I looked a lot better in those days," or "I really look better today than I did back then," or "Did I really look like that?" Often times, the basis for any of these impressions is a reaction to your hairstyle.

For the fortunate men who have a full head of hair, be sure your cut and style compliment your specific facial features and structure. You may wish to look at some of the hairstyle options that are pictured in magazines found in most salons and barber shops. If you do decide to change your hairstyle, we recommend that you first consult with your stylist or barber for a professional opinion.

Your hair influences your image in more ways than just the cut or style you have. The color of your hair is also very important. Don't be afraid to modify your hair color. Women have been doing it for centuries and now men are becoming more accepting of this practice. Many women may say that grey hair on a man looks "distinguished" yet they spend a fortune every year to insure that no grey is seen on *their* own heads. Much like baldness, grey hair is sometimes perceived as an indication of being "over the hill." Of course there are exceptional individuals, such as actors John Forsythe or Cary Grant, who look outstanding with grey hair, but even Cary Grant did not allow his grey to show in his films until he reached his late fifties. Unfortunately, most of us do not look like Forsythe or Grant, and in order to make a living and compete in the world, we must avail ourselves of every advantage.

Grey hair can be very attractive on many a man, depending on his facial structure and the particular shade of grey. But grey hair that has a yellowish cast or grey on a balding head are decidedly less appealing.

There certainly are circumstances when grey hair is an asset: for example, if a man looks too young, a little grey hair can help him project an image of maturity. We know of one case in which a man in search of a new position in sales had his dark hair highlighted with grey to create a salt and pepper look. We don't know if his hair was the deciding factor but he got the job.

HAIR COLORING

Contrary to popular belief, stress or worry does not cause hair to turn grey. Hair color comes from a pigment called *melanin*, which is produced by the cells at the base of the hair shafts. This same pigment makes all hair colors: a little melanin and you're a blond; a lot of it produces darker hair color shades. As you get older these cells (also called *melanocytes*) stop producing melanin, and as a result your hair gradually becomes grey or white. People don't just turn grey overnight.

If you look great in grey, shampoos such as Great Looking Grey® will enhance your color by eliminating any signs of yellowing and bring out its natural shine. But if you still wish that your melanocytes were going strong, then show your colors. In the past the only option available to men who were not pleased with their grey hair was to use a woman's hair-coloring product that took more than a half hour to set because of the chemical process involved. Image Enhancement Technology has responded to this problem: today we have hair-coloring products designed specifically for men. One such product is called Just For Men® Shampoo-in Haircolor, which can be shampooed in and rinsed out after a few minutes. It blends away grey and looks very natural. The color lasts up to six weeks. Just look for the shade you desire by checking the color indicator on each box. Another product, Grecian Plus®, thickens and conditions the hair while gradually restoring its color. In fact, Grecian Formula® works very much like melanin. A smaller amount restores hair to a lighter tone. More of the formula brings hair back to a natural-looking darker shade.

Years ago men had to live with their grey hair; now you have choices. Some of you like your silver lining; others, who feel too young to be old, view the new hair products made just for them as brighter alternatives.

According to psychologist Dr. Ross Goldstein, founder of Generation Insights, a California consulting firm, and a Harvard Ph.D., "Growing facial hair is an accessible and socially acceptable way to express one's masculinity in the '90s." Over the years, the areas in which men can express their maleness have been reduced,

Oakland Athletics Hall of Fame pitching star Rollie Fingers covers his grey hair (*left*) and maintains his youthful image (*right*) by using hair color. (Photographs courtesy of Combe, Inc., Just For Men® Shampoo-in Haircolor)

but "this is one area that is uniquely male." Many young and middle-aged men grow beards because they can. According to anthropologists and psychologists, growing facial hair is one of the few remaining things that a man can do and almost all women can't.

For decades the popularity of facial hair had been on the decline. Then in the 1960s men once again began sporting facial hair, and now more than thirty-five million men have facial hair in the form of mustaches, beards, or sideburns.

All mustaches and beards go through that really nasty stage when you will be tempted to get out the razor. Getting there is not half the fun. The first two weeks are the worst. Avoid the desire to scratch if your skin begins to itch—and it will. Use a facial moisturizer to cool down these little tickles. Hint: moisturizing works best after a shower.

Your facial hair may grow in but be a different color than your hair or it may grow in uneven or patchy. It is not at all unusual for facial hair to be darker than the hair on your head. Facial hair can also be tricky because it can signal the passing of time: it's where grey hair usually shows up first. The good news is that if you can handle a toothbrush and are willing to invest five minutes of your time, Just For Men® Brush-in Color Gel for Mustache, Beard, and Sideburns, is formulated specifically for facial hair to create a surprising match with your hair color.

Tips on Coloring Your Hair

One way to test how a change of hair color will look on you is to try a rinse before you use a more permanent hair-coloring process. Rinses are available in most shades and can be purchased at drug stores and beauty supply outlets. A rinse will only last through three or four washings, but using one will give you a preview of how a change of color will affect your image. The following is a list of other recommendations that you should consider when coloring your hair, beard, or mustache.

Photographer George Hiotis before and after a complete hair coloring. (Photographs courtesy of Combe, Inc., Just For Men® Shampoo-in Haircolor and Just For Men® Brush-in Color Gel for Mustache, Beard, and Sideburns. Photographed by Dirck Halstead.)

- It's always better to try a shade lighter than you think you need. For instance, if you think your hair is dark brown, try the next lighter shade (e.g., medium brown) the first time. You can always go darker.

- As you get older your complexion can change tone. As a rule of thumb, the older you get the lighter your complexion, and the lighter your hair color should be.

- Don't be in a rush. Read and follow the package directions carefully. Adhering to the directions and the suggested timing will produce the best results.

- If you would like to leave a little grey at your temples or in your beard or sideburns, you can control the end result: just brush in the coloring gel where you want it.

HAIR LOSS

Even the biggest stars in Hollywood are not excluded from the scourge suffered by millions of men, namely, hair loss. As in the case of your height and sometimes your weight, hair loss (when and where you loose it) is predetermined by genetics. The only exception to genetic hair loss is that caused by illness, chemotherapy, and certain viral or bacterial conditions, but even these causes of hair loss are usually temporary.

Despite what people may say, each of us perceives a man differently depending upon whether or not the person we are viewing has a head of hair. Could the bald Sean Connery have ever created the character of the dashing, womanizing British agent James Bond without his hairpiece? Of course not. Very few people would imagine women falling all over some guy with no hair. We imagine that men with hair have much more exciting lives than those without. To take this a little further, could a bald William Shatner be Captain Kirk, commander of the Starship Enterprise, without his hairpiece? Would Burt Reynolds have been a leading man for more than a decade? You can bet there would never have been a *Smokey and the Bandit* without Burt's hair.

Corporate mogul Donald Trump is quoted in John C. O'Donnell's book *Trumped* as saying, "Baldness is a sign of weakness." For Trump it appears that image equals reality. He is also quoted as saying, "The worst thing a man can do is to let himself go bald." Contrary to this opinion, there are several organizations promoting the idea that bald is beautiful, and for some men this may be true. Baldness was one of the trademarks of stars such as Yul Brynner and Telly Savalas. Some viewers considered them sex symbols, but this is the exception not the rule. For most men, their self-esteem recedes along with their hairline.

While many men accept their baldness and learn to live with it, others look in the mirror and believe a statement attributed to Woody Allen: "My only regret in life is that I am not someone else." The day has arrived when you no longer have to wish you were somebody else. By utilizing the tools provided by Image Enhancement Technology you can become more of who you really are.

TRANSPLANTS

Hair transplanting is basically just introducing hair to areas of the scalp where it is no longer present. The first step in deciding whether you are a candidate for a hair transplant is a consultation with your doctor. If it is determined that a transplant is a viable option for you, contact a board certified plastic surgeon. These professionals have been successfully performing this procedure for more than thirty years.

An individual with very little hair might not be advised to undergo hair replacement surgery. Transplant candidates must have healthy hair growth at the

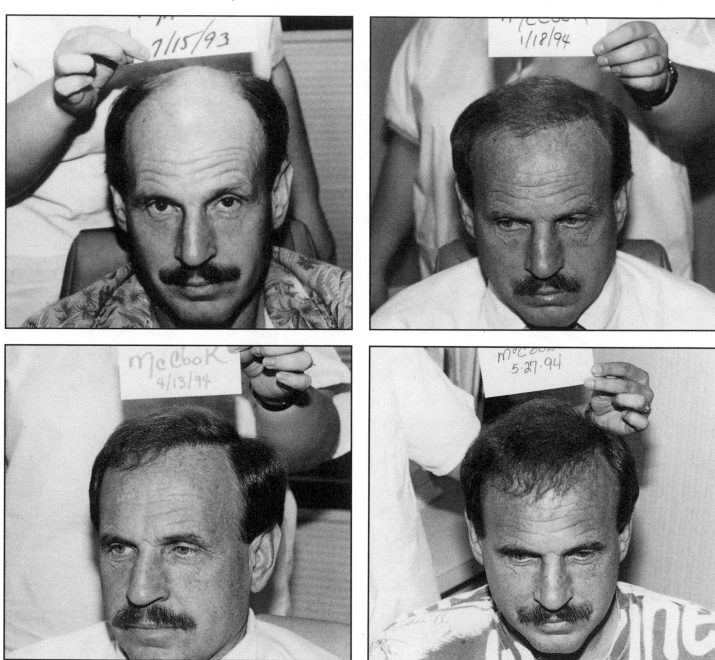

These photographs illustrate the progress of a combination scalp reduction and transplant. (Courtesy of *Alpha*-OMEGA HAIR & SCALP CLINICS, Tampa, Florida)

back and sides of the head to serve as donor areas from which the grafts and flaps are taken. Other factors such as hair texture, color, curliness, or waviness may affect the cosmetic result. There are a number of techniques used in hair replacement surgery and sometimes two or more of these procedures are used to achieve the desired results.

Transplant techniques, which can be explained in depth by your surgeon, include a variety of procedures such as punch grafts, mini grafts, and strip grafts, which are generally performed on patients who desire a more modest change in the fullness of their hair or wish to fill in a receding hairline. Flaps, tissue expansion, and scalp reduction are procedures more appropriate for patients who desire a more dramatic change. After the initial surgery, most men require a touch up procedure that adds to or evens out the hair to finalize the natural looking result.

CHEMICAL TREATMENT: TOPICAL SOLUTION

The prescription drug Rogaine®, manufactured by the Upjohn Pharmaceutical Company, has produced outstanding results on some individuals and is the first, and presently the only, product medically proven to grow hair. Most men loose their hair due to a progressive shrinking or miniaturization of the hair follicles. This causes a shortening of the hair's growing cycle. Over time the active growing phase becomes shorter and the resting stage becomes longer until eventually there is no growth at all. Rogaine® works in part by partially reversing the miniaturization process. This prolongs the growth phase providing improved coverage of the scalp. Upjohn Company, the manufacturer of Rogaine®, offers a free consultation with a dermatologist to determine if their product can help you with your hair-loss problem. For more information, call toll free (800) 635-0655. It could make a difference in your life.

REPLACEMENT

Hair weaves are hair replacements marketed as being "semi-permanent replacements." The hair-weaving procedure involves sewing the hair replacement unit on to existing hair. Since the existing hair will continue to grow, the weave will become loose and has to be tightened regularly. The weave may offer an answer to the man with hair loss on the top of his head but who still retains good growth on the sides and back. It is also virtually impossible to pull off a hair weave because it is intertwined with your own hair. These weaves are so secure that they can be worn by professional athletes during competition.

According to *Forbes* magazine, American men now spend $350 million a year on hair replacement. One of the major beneficiaries of this trend is Sy Sperling, now famous for television commercials for his Hair Club for Men ("I'm not just the president, I'm also a client"). The Sy Sperling story is another example of transforming an image to transform a life.

In 1968, Sperling was a swimming pool salesman smoking three packs of cigarettes a day and drinking about ten cups of coffee. To make matters worse, he had lost most of his hair and was thirty-five pounds overweight. That same year Sperling and his first wife decided to get a divorce. For the first time in years he found himself thrust into the singles scene. Because of his circumstances and his physical appearance, he had lost his self-esteem and his self-confidence.

Sperling knew that his balding, overweight image was having a negative impact on his life, and he was determined to do something about it. The first thing he did was to get a hair replacement unit. When he saw the amazing difference it made in his image, he was motivated to change his entire lifestyle. He quit smoking and became a vegetarian. He also began exercising and, in time, the bloated, bald Sy Sperling made business history.

Sperling eventually remarried and together with his second wife, Amy, who is a hairdresser, he opened a small salon in Manhattan. Dissatisfied with traditional hairpieces, Sperling purchased a hair replacement system from inventor Walter

Sy Sperling before and after his hair replacement. (Photographs courtesy of Hair Club For Men, Ltd.)

Tucciarone. But Sperling credits Amy with inventing the hair club system. "She took a basic concept and, through trial and error, perfected it to create a superior product." Sy Sperling has become a multimillionaire by marketing his "strand by strand" hair replacement system on television.

Unlike the old-style toupees, Image Enhancement Technology offers a poly-urethane-type material that is invisible when placed over the skin. This material serves as the base for the hair replacement, so that it looks like the hair is growing right out of the scalp. Another feature of the technically improved hair replacement is that it can be attached semi-permanently thus removing worries that often accompany the wearing of a hairpiece. Has it occurred to you that you don't notice as many hairpieces on men anymore? The fact is, there about five times as many men wearing hair replacements today than in 1975. Technology has perfected the visual aspects of hair replacements to the point that, today, they are virtually undetectable.

Thanks to the superior type of hair replacements being offered by Sperling's Hair Club For Men and all of the excellent independent hair replacement specialists, the days of the "rug toupee" are over. Bald men have been searching for hair-loss remedies since the beginning of time. We are lucky to be living in a world where Image Enhancement Technology offers men the first real undetectable solu-tion to hair loss.

We can promise you one thing: life is very short and you will get old soon enough, so there is no need to help it along. We know there are some men who take comfort in hiding behind a grey, balding, overweight image. But for those of you who want to remain competitive and live life to its fullest, only being your very best will be good enough.

If what some scientists say is true, we humans make use of about 10 percent of our brain's capacity. The same point could also be said about our image. Most men, through positive attitude, exercise, diet, and utilizing Image Enhancement Technologies can improve their image significantly. This is not unnatural, it is utilizing every opportunity to be the very best that you can be.

Image Enhancement Technologies of hair color and surgical or nonsurgical hair replacements can raise your Image Quotient 1 to 2 points.

12

The Eyes Have It

EYEGLASSES

Many men do not have perfect vision so they must compensate for this by utilizing the advanced technology offered by today's optical lenses. There are still some men who feel that wearing eyeglasses communicates weakness. Consider this story about the reluctance to wear glasses featuring the dashing and debonair screen star Rex Harrison. As the story goes, Harrison had very poor eyesight but would never allow himself to be seen or photographed wearing his glasses. He always arranged it so that someone else (usually a young lady) would drive his Rolls Royce through the studio gates to a spot where Rex felt comfortable that there would be no photographers around to capture his secret on film. When he drove his car through the studio gates by himself, he navigated largely on memory and instinct.

In years gone by eyeglasses were thought by some to be a sign of weakness. A youngster wearing glasses might have been given the nickname "four eyes." The wearing of glasses also proved to be an impediment to participating in some athletic games. But in recent years the fickle world of fashion has taken a new turn. Today eyeglasses can constitute a fashion statement. They have become so popular that some men who do not require them wear glasses fitted with plain lenses. One of the reasons for this surge in the popularity of glasses is that they can make you *look* smarter. We are moving out of the industrial age and into

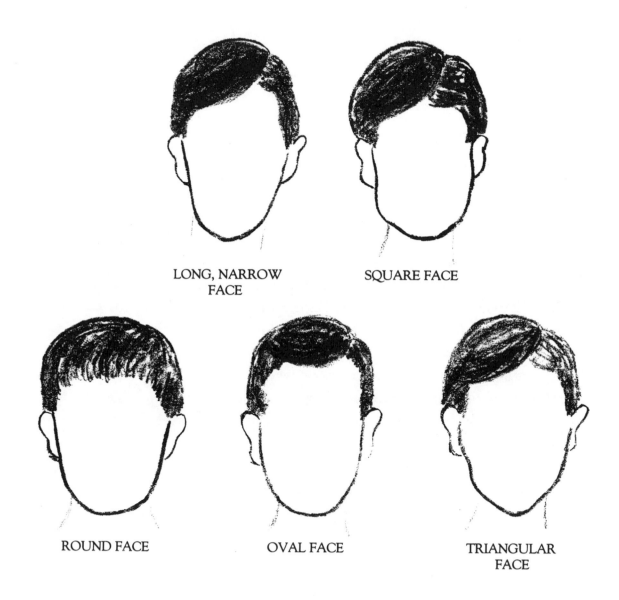

LONG, NARROW
FACE

SQUARE FACE

ROUND FACE

OVAL FACE

TRIANGULAR
FACE

Whether your face is long and narrow, square, triangular, round, or oval, a skilled optician can find
the right size and shape of eyeglasses to fit your prescription and compliment your face. Sometimes

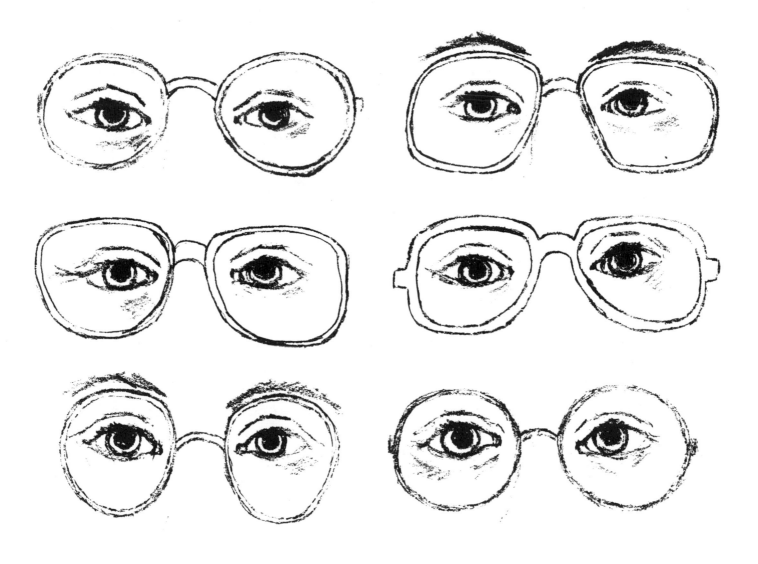

all it takes is a well-chosen style of eyewear to reduce the affect of a thin or a very round face, high cheekbones, crow's-feet, eyes that are too close together or too far apart, or any number of irregularities. (Illustrations courtesy of Shirley Lombardo)

the information age, where intelligence is becoming even more important to a successful image. Intelligence in this world of technology is the key to survival as well as success.

Today we have a multitude of frames and lenses from which to choose. In addition, the invention of the plastic lens offers a lightweight alternative to thick, heavy glass lenses and eliminates the hazard posed by broken or shattered spectacles. The use of plastic lenses has extended the careers of many professional athletes; moreover, today's eyeglass frames offer a wide variety of styles and shapes. The right selection of frames complement the primary facial structures and can actually overcome many common facial irregularities.

CONTACT LENSES

The technology for improving vision reached new heights with the advent of contact lenses. Instead of bulky and cumbersome eyeglasses, many people were prescribed small lenses that are placed directly on the cornea of the eye. These lenses dramatically improve vision by reducing the work each lens has to perform in order to aid in focusing an image on the retina. The first versions of contacts were solid and had to be carefully placed and positioned to prevent scratching the surface of the eye. Since their arrival contacts have become less expensive and are now made of pliable materials, which has improved their comfort and popularity.

Some people feel that they would look better if their eyes were a different color. If you have brown eyes but you wish they were blue, Image Enhancement Technology can make this wish come true through the use of tinted contact lenses.

Unlike the old-fashioned hard lenses, today's newest contacts are custom fitted. Many people have tried to wear contact lenses but found that their eyes became irritated or the lenses lost their shape over time. Contacts can't improve your total look if they irritate your eyes and are uncomfortable to wear. Many of the newer lenses are made from materials that allow oxygen to enter your cornea and prevent irritation. There are even disposable contact lenses that require no maintenance such as soaking in antibacterial moisturizing solutions. (Note: If you do wear contact lenses, it is strongly advised that you wear sunglasses during exposure to bright sunlight.)

SUNGLASSES

Ultraviolet B (UVB) rays are the dark side of sunlight. Along with causing sunburn and skin cancer these UVB rays can cause keratitis, something like a sunburn on the front of the eye. Symptoms include a reddening of the front of the eye and the eyelids; a sensation of "sand" in the eyes; excessive tearing; and, often, an extreme sensitivity to light. UVB rays can also contribute to the formation of cataracts, a clouding of the lens of the eye. People with blue, green, or other light-colored eyes are at higher risk for UVB damage. The harmful effects of UVB rays can be either immediate or cumulative so beware, exposure to these rays today can cause problems tomorrow. The fact that UVB rays may damage your eyes does not mean that you have to spend the rest of your life with the window shades drawn. Medical experts agree that the correct and consistent wearing of quality sunglasses that block the rays will decrease the likelihood of eye damage from the sun. Research by eyewear companies such as Bausch and Lomb, the makers of Ray-Ban® sunglasses, developed lenses that filter out the harmful effects of UVB.

Beyond the issue of eye protection, the new frame designs and lens coloring available for sunglasses can make a strong fashion statement. Whatever your mood, whatever the occasion, sunglasses can be a valuable image accessory.

Faces come in all shapes and colors; that's why sunglasses are made in so many styles. Using the line of your eyebrows is a good indicator of the type

Sunglasses can make a strong fashion statement. (Photograph courtesy of Michael and Walter Mocellin, and Barbizon Academy of Ontario, Canada)

of frame that will flow with the shape of your face. If you are not able to determine what style looks best on you, we recommend that you go with the classic aviator or "goggle shape"; they look good on just about every man. It's difficult to find a picture of the late General Douglas MacArthur without his aviator sunglasses on. He may have believed they enhanced his image as a leader.

ELECTROLYSIS

Just as eyeglass frames can be very important in bringing out the best qualities of your face, your eyebrows—an area of the face usually neglected by most men— can greatly affect the expression projected by your eyes. Thick, bushy eyebrows can create a sinister or lecherous look. If your eyebrows are growing together or do not have good separation, it can distort your total appearance.

The best and most permanent solution to thick, heavy eyebrows is *electrolysis*, the removal of hair using electrical current to destroy the roots. When performed by a trained professional this procedure can reshape your eyebrows to upgrade your image. Electrolysis provides a permanent solution to the problem of unwanted hair. A mild current of electricity is used to remove the hair by destroying the papilla (the source of nourishment for the hair follicle). With this method the possibility of regeneration is less than 15 percent.

Utilizing the Image Enhancement Technology for the eyes offered by today's eyeglasses, contact lenses, sunglasses, and electrolysis can significantly raise your Image Quotient.

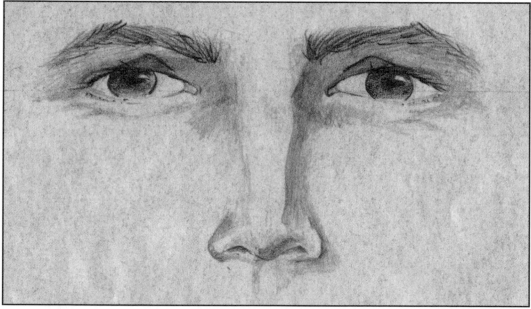

Above: Before electrolysis, hair intrudes on the bridge of the nose and the eyebrows are bushy and ill-defined. *Below*: After electroloysis, there is a more contoured look, with the nose and eyebrows set apart as distinctive features of the face. (Illustrations courtesy of Heather Harvey)

13

The Million-Dollar Smile

GIVING GOOD VIBES

Back in the 1960s someone who had the effect of lifting your spirits or who instilled a sense of trust was often described as giving off good vibrations (frequently shortened to "vibes"). Conversely when meeting someone who makes you feel negative or suspicious, they were described as giving off bad vibrations. While such vibes don't literally emanate from others it is a fact that we all experience definite and almost immediate feelings about the people we meet: for example, they are confident or uncertain, smart or ignorant, good or bad, sincere or phony.

Self-esteem is one of the most important elements of the human experience: it is vital for emotional, mental, and physical well-being. Positive self-esteem generates a feeling of confidence. The quality of possessing a healthy self-confidence (not to be confused with arrogance) can be sensed by others. People are much more apt to like a man who likes himself. A man who exudes self-confidence is readily accepted as a leader. A strong feeling of self-confidence is needed to win not only in athletic competition, but also in business and in many areas of your personal life.

Self-confidence generates self-esteem and these may well be two of the most important requisite ingredients in the formula for happiness and success in life. Self-esteem reflects "how you see yourself," and one of the important ingredients in the development of a man's self-esteem is his self-image.

Paying attention to your physical image does not mean being narcissistic or placing the way you look above all other things in life. On the contrary, it is a means rather than an end. It is a powerful tool that can enable you to attain those truly important things all of us seek.

In a recent poll taken of corporate executives it was found that more than 85 percent were within their normal weight range and more than 70 percent were at least five feet, ten inches tall. Does this group tend to be tall and close to ideal weight because its members are corporate executives or were they chosen for their positions as executives in part because of these image factors? It takes little knowledge of, or insight into, the business world to realize how much importance is placed on both corporate and individual image.

All the food you consume and to a great extent all the air you breathe enters your body through the mouth. Besides being a vital orifice for life-giving nourishment, your mouth is also one of the most sensuous parts of your body. Many physical intimacies can be exchanged orally, kissing being one of the most popular. How often have you heard someone say, "I couldn't resist his smile." In many polls a person's smile has been rated as the feature most noted by people who meet someone for the first time. Greeting the world with stained or crooked teeth can destroy an otherwise excellent appearance. The luster of white teeth is an indication of a healthy lifestyle, which is a key factor in the overall image of a successful man.

THE HISTORY OF SMILE TECHNOLOGY

Considerable progress has been made in the field of dentistry since the dentists of ancient Greece crafted teeth from bone and tied them to adjacent teeth with gold wire. Around 700 B.C.E. the Romans replaced missing teeth with wooden ones inserted directly into the empty socket. These replacement teeth were made of boxwood, a type of wood that would swell in the socket making them stable in the mouth.

After the Middle Ages, noblemen and other wealthy Europeans could select from a wide array of false teeth and dentures. Since cost was not an issue for the upper classes, teeth were crafted from silver, mother of pearl (hence the phrase "pearly whites"), or enameled copper and attached to an ivory base. For people of rank, the wearing of such teeth, crafted in fine materials, was as fashionable as the jewelry they possessed. These precious dentures gave new meaning to the phrase "million-dollar smile."

The transplanting of teeth from one person to another became popular in the seventeenth century. A decaying tooth was pulled from the socket and immediately replaced with a healthy tooth pulled from another mouth. This seemingly barbaric procedure actually worked, often the transplanted tooth would settle down in the socket within four to six weeks and remain there indefinitely. This method became very popular during the eighteenth century, so the poor were encouraged to sell their healthy teeth to satisfy the demand. By the end of the nineteenth century the procedure of transplanting teeth was replaced by technological innovations in the science of tooth replacement.

Today there are a multitude of products that will give you a whiter, brighter smile and healthier teeth and gums. We have grown well beyond tooth powders for cleaning teeth. Now there are formulas containing ingredients for tartar control and fighting plaque. There are baking soda and fluoride-enriched formulas in the form of pastes, powders, and gels. In many cases it requires more than personal dental care to attain a million-dollar smile. What follows is a summary of the options that are available to enhance your smile.

BONDING OR VENEERING

Incredible progress has been made in the field of cosmetic dentistry. You no longer have to avoid smiling because you are uncomfortable with the way your teeth look. Maybe there is a gap between your teeth or they are badly stained. Maybe you have been avoiding having that chipped tooth repaired. With the aid of an increasingly popular and effective dental technique known as *bonding,* these concerns have become a thing of the past. Bonding with composite resins and laminate veneers can immediately upgrade the quality of your smile. This process can fill in gaps between your teeth, restore color, and even make your teeth look straighter.

In many cases bonding can be used to treat teeth that are chipped or fractured. "Bonding" is a general term that describes a variety of techniques. Each of these methods involves attaching or bonding a plastic or porcelain material to the existing tooth surface. Bonding can also be used to restore decayed teeth and for crowning teeth. It can also protect exposed roots and seal the degenerated tooth from further decay.

ENAMEL SHAPING

Enamel shaping is a process of contouring natural teeth to improve their appearance. This process can be used when your teeth become uneven or your eye teeth (the sharp pointed teeth) appear to be too long. Enamel shaping involves modifying your teeth by removing or contouring enamel to create harmony and balance to the mouth.

CROWNS

A crown is a restorative process that covers or caps a tooth to reconstruct its normal shape and size. Its purpose is to strengthen or improve the appearance of a tooth. Crowns should be considered to support a large filling where there isn't enough tooth remaining to protect weak teeth from fracturing, and to cover badly shaped or discolored teeth. The application of this technology could restore your teeth to their natural beauty.

IMPLANTS

Today dental implants are coming a step closer to providing artificial teeth that look natural and feel secure. Implants attach artificial teeth directly to the jaw. There are three components to an implant:

(1) An anchor is placed into the jawbone. Bone then grows around the anchor holding it firmly in place.

(2) A post is attached to the anchor (the post connects the anchor to the artificial tooth).

(3) The artificial tooth is attached to the anchor.

Implants entail a complex procedure requiring specific knowledge and training. If you are considering a dental implant, consult your dentist for complete information and possibly a referral.

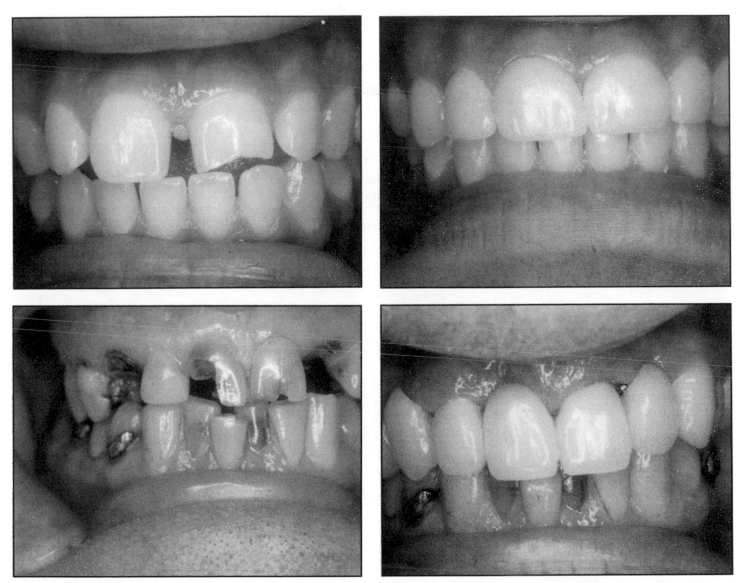

Upper left: A patient's teeth before bonding is applied. *Upper right*: The same patient after bonding has corrected the chipped tooth and the gap in the front teeth. *Lower left*: A patient's teeth before bonding and dental implants. *Lower right*: The same patient after these procedures. (Photographs courtesy of The Aesthetics Associates Centre, Amherst, New York)

BRIDGES AND DENTURES

We have come a very long way since the days of George Washington and his wooden teeth. Bridges seem to be well named because they serve to "bridge" the gap to a new smile. A bridge is actually a partial denture that comes in two types—fixed and removable. Removable bridges can be taken out for cleaning but are not generally as stable in the mouth as the fixed variety. If you are missing some teeth, a bridge will help maintain the natural shape of your face and may help support your lips and cheeks. The loss of back teeth may cause your mouth to sink in and make your face look older. Missing teeth can also affect the way you chew and speak. Dentures of one form or another have been in use for more than two thousand years, however, these substitutes for missing teeth have never been as effective, as easy to use, or as appealing as they are today.

TEETH STRAIGHTENING

One very common dental problem affecting your image is crooked teeth. This problem is much easier to correct if it is taken care of during the childhood years. The fitting of dental braces, or in less severe cases dental retainers, offers a solution by gradually shifting the teeth into their proper place. The shifting process may take up to one year and requires ongoing adjustments to the braces or retainers. It is a slow, gradual process and somewhat inconvenient but the results can be well worth the effort.

BLEACHING

Bleaching is a procedure designed to brighten teeth that are discolored. A chemical oxidizing solution is applied to the teeth and activated by heat or a combination of heat and light. Generally only three or four visits to your dentist are necessary to restore a brilliant smile.

One of the newest do-it-yourself cosmetic dental systems is a tooth whitening system called Bright 'N' Natural®. This system was created by two brothers, Todd and Samuel Shatkin, the former a dentist and the latter a plastic surgeon. The system includes a professional quality whitening paste that is brushed on in the conventional manner. The kit also includes a whitening gel that is applied in conjunction with two dental trays (mouthpieces) that you can custom form to fit over both your upper and lower teeth. During the treatment the contoured dental trays act as holders for the gel. This system is much more comfortable, less costly, and just as effective as the bleaching that a dentist would do. Utilizing this system can restore your smile and brighten your image.

If you feel that your smile could be improved by any of these procedures, put your money where your mouth is. The utilization of the Image Enhancement Technology of cosmetic dentistry will definitely raise your Image Quotient.

14

Plastic Surgery

BEAUTY AND THE BEAST

During his teenage years coauthor Richard Derwald spent some time working as a professional wrestler. The ongoing success of professional wrestling is based on little more than a parade of images reflecting the good and evil in our society. The post Vietnam war period was one in which anything military was perceived as evil and brutal. During this dove period a man calling himself Sergeant Slaughter became a top box office villain in the wrestling world. Later, when problems began bubbling up in the Middle East, another personality known as the Iron Sheik (from Iran of course) emerged as the most hated of wrestling opponents. Sergeant Slaughter then became a "good guy" and his matches with the Iron Sheik drew great crowds. In this world of pessimism, kids and many adults needed a hero figure, and professional wrestling with all its flaws provided it in the form of six foot, five inch, blond-haired, blue-eyed "Hulk" Hogan. When the Hulk defeated the Iron Sheik to win the World Wrestling Federation championship, it reassured the fans that our country could overcome any threat.

When Richard was active in wrestling back in the 1950s, there was a standing joke that the promoters were still fighting the Second World War and the Cold War at the same time. The "good guys" had to have an "All-American" look. What the promoters really wanted were young wrestlers, or "baby faces" as they were called in the business. These were men who looked like the type that every

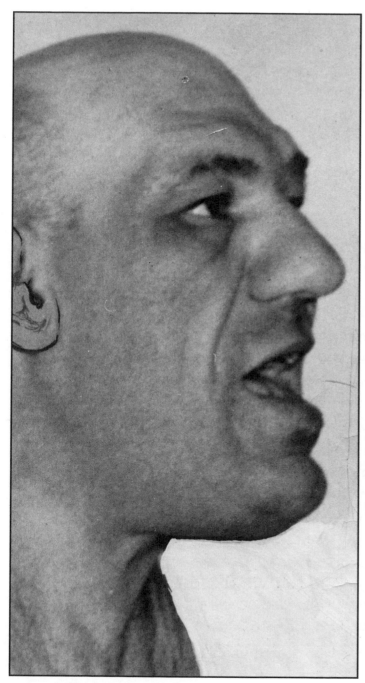

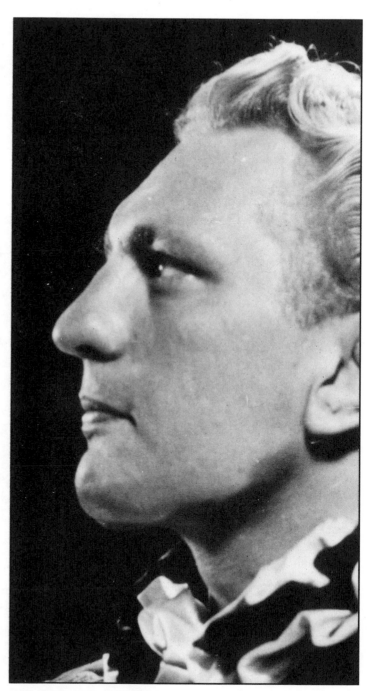

Mauriece Tillet, "The French Angel"

"Nature Boy" Buddy Rogers

mother wanted her daughter to marry. They could be the ideal brother, son, or husband, and it was their job while in the ring to protect and defend virtue, honor, and the American way.

Back then, if you wanted to succeed as a "bad guy" you had to construct an image of a foreign menace from the past or present. Naturally the most successful bad guy images were German, Japanese, and Russian. Some successful Germans were Fritz von Erich and Hans Hermann. The most hated, and therefore the most successful, of the group took the name of Hans Schmidt, who was really a French Canadian from Quebec. Before he shaved his head, he started his career wrestling as a baby face called Guy LaRose. There were Russians such as Ivan Rasputian and Ivan and Karol Kalmakoff. Karol was a bodybuilder from New Jersey whose real name was Karol Kauser. The ranks of the Japanese included Mr. Moto and Tosh Togo, who was really Harold Sakata, an Olympic weight lifter from Hawaii.

The ideal match, from a box office perspective, was to bring together a super villain, such as the evil Hans Schmidt, and an American superhero like Olympic medal winner Verne Gange. Another box office bonanza that played extremely well all over America was the "Beauty and the Beast." This surefire attraction matched the blond, handsome, and muscular "Nature Boy" Buddy Rogers against a human gargoyle named Mauriece Tillet, who called himself "The French Angel."

"Nature Boy" was a former cop from Camden, New Jersey, whose real name was Herman Rodes, known to his friends as "Dutch." Mauriece Tillet was a Frenchman afflicted with a glandular disorder that caused his head to swell to more than twice its normal size, distorting all his facial features. The disease also caused Tillet's hairy body to take on freakish proportions, with long arms and huge hands. The visual contrast between the images of these two men was incredible: every time the deformed gargoyle would kick or appear to hurt the sun-bronzed Nature Boy, women would cover their eyes in horror. When the Nature Boy turned the tables and got the best of his opponent, the crowd went crazy. It was as if all the ugly brutality in the world was being purged.

When Richard had the pleasure of meeting Mauriece Tillet on two occasions, the wrestler's physical appearance belied his true nature. Tillet was probably one of the kindest, most gentle people imaginable. Everyone in the wrestling business knew that Mauriece was brilliant, some might have even considered him a scholar. The throngs of fans who paid to jeer and taunt him every night made their decision about who he was based on the way he looked (after all, that's human nature) and on how he was promoted. Mauriece Tillet turned a physical affliction into a career, and made a great deal of money at it. Although he always seemed at peace with the world, it no doubt bothered a man of his intellect to make his living as little more than a sideshow curiosity.

One last story about images and wrestling. One of the legends of the ring is "Gorgeous George," a former professional boxer whose real name was George Wagner. His early years in wrestling proved to be a major disappointment, so he found himself working in what was called the "tank town circuit" of small-town events. One day he was booked to wrestle at a VFW hall in Ohio. He arrived two days before the event because he did not have any prior bookings. When he arrived in town the promoter told him that there might not be a show because so few tickets were sold. The promoter then asked if there was anything George could do to pump up ticket sales.

George went back to his small hotel room and racked his brain to come up with a gimmick that would sell tickets. He was just about broke and needed some money to get to his next booking. Then a brilliant idea came to him. The next morning he called the local newspaper and told them that one of the wrestlers on the Saturday night show had an appointment for a permanent wave and hair color at a local beauty parlor that day. Remember, this was 1946, a time when men went to barber shops, not beauty parlors. The newspaper jumped on the story, and brought a photographer to take a picture of this wrestler. The photographer found George in the chair with his newly colored blonde hair in curling rods. After the story with the picture captioned "Meet George the wrestler, isn't he gorgeous?" was published in the newspaper, the VFW hall was sold out. There was a standing room only crowd. This clever gimmick turned George Wagner, a down and out wrestler, into one of the greatest box office attractions in the history of professional wrestling. George Wagner became a world renowned personality known as "The Human Orchid," Gorgeous George.

The box-office attraction of Gorgeous George came from his self-characterization as an effeminate man. The fans flocked in when he was matched up against the "All-American" male heroes. What they were experiencing was the power of physical imagery; the real George Wagner was in no way effeminate. Many of the wrestlers of that time strongly resented what George was doing. They felt his act was bad for the business. According to one popular story, one night in Buffalo, Gorgeous George was scheduled to meet another tough guy who called himself "Strangler" Bob Wagner. After the preliminary matches were underway in the packed auditorium, the promoter came into the Strangler's dressing room to give him his instructions on how and when to lose the match with the Gorgeous one. When Strangler found out that he was supposed to lose, he became enraged. The promoter explained that George was a national attraction and his contract stipulated that he would always win his matches. The Strangler indicated that Gorgeous George would either defeat him fairly or be beaten himself. The promoter rushed to George's dressing room and described the situation. George agreed. The match between these two was a brutal slug fest in which George's experience as a professional boxer proved to be too much for the Strangler, who left the ring bloodied with a broken nose and several broken ribs.

Although he should have known better, Strangler Bob Wagner believed what he saw: that Gorgeous George, with his blonde curls and arched eyebrows, was weak and vulnerable. The Strangler made a very important career decision based on another person's image, just as most other human beings would do. What we see becomes reality in our minds. George Wagner enhanced his career by intentionally creating the image of a sissy while in reality he was a very tough, gutsy guy. (You had to be to do what he did!)

By modifying your physical image you have the power to influence how people relate to you.

PLASTIC SURGERY

The term "plastic surgery" was derived from the Greek word *plastikos*, which means "molded" or "giving form." History suggests that the practice of plastic surgery has ancient roots but the technology of today's reconstructive surgeons had its beginnings in the nineteenth-century royal courts of Europe. According to John Santino, director of the Alpha-Omega Hair Replacement Clinic in Largo, Florida, many members of royal families availed themselves of a new surgical procedure that pulled the skin of the face upward and then surgically removed the folded excess skin, hiding the surgical scar in the patients' hairline or under a wig. This procedure was the first form of a facelift. Because the skin was pulled upward this procedure tended to move the eyebrows up and away from their normal position on the face. Since these early procedures were extremely expensive only royalty or the very rich could afford facelifts. These were the same people who attended the opera, the theater, and had the education to comprehend advanced literary works. Because of the great popularity of the facelift among this elite group, a new term came into being, "high brow."

Today, scientific advances in the field of plastic surgery allow practitioners to achieve improvements in human form and function that were thought impossible only ten years ago. The medical speciality of plastic surgery, dedicated to restoring and reshaping the human body, is defined by the American Medical Association and the American Society of Plastic and Reconstructive Surgeons as:

(1) Reconstructive surgery to correct problems of abnormal body structure caused by birth defects, injuries, infection, tumors, or disease.

(2) Cosmetic surgery to reshape or restore normal structures of the body to improve appearance and self-esteem.

Because society places such a high value on men and women looking young and fit, a growing percentage of those who now request plastic surgery are male. The types of surgical procedures they request are often not the same as those sought by women. This is particularly true when it comes to body contouring, since men tend to develop fat deposits in different parts of their bodies. The procedure used to remove localized fat deposits is called *liposuction*. While not a substitute for proper weight reduction, it is a method of removing localized fat that does not respond to diet or exercise. In a man's body these unwanted fat deposits usually occur around the abdomen and waist or around the chin and neck.

Liposuction consists of suctioning (sucking out) the fat of the body through a small hollow tube inserted via one or more tiny incisions. These incisions are usually hidden in the natural body creases and leave nearly imperceptible scars. The best candidates for liposuction are men of relatively normal weight with isolated pockets of fat. It is also important that candidates have firm, elastic skin. Loose and drooping skin won't reshape to your body's new contours; it may even require additional surgical procedures to remove the excess skin. This procedure *will* leave visible scars.

There is another body contouring procedure that is used to correct a condition affecting an estimated 40 to 60 percent of the male population, especially those over fifty years of age. This condition is called *gynecomastia*, a medical term rooted in the Greek words for "woman-like breasts." There are certain medical conditions and drugs that can cause enlarged breasts in men, but for the vast majority of cases there is no known cause. This problem (not to be confused with muscular pectorals developed through exercise) is primarily cosmetic, causing embarrassment in the locker room and on the beach. If you're uncomfortable with the size of your breasts, chances are a plastic surgeon can help. If your gynecomastia consists primarily of excessive fatty tissue, your surgeon will probably remove it using liposuction. If your breast enlargement is caused by glandular tissue, the excess tissue will probably be cut out, sometimes in conjunction with liposuction. Surgery for gynecomastia may be done as an outpatient procedure or with an overnight hospital stay. It may be performed under general or local anesthesia, and usually the procedure takes about an hour and a half to complete.

Why Would You Have It Done?

A man's motivation to have plastic surgery is sometimes different from a woman's. The decision may revolve around one issue, career advancement. Men also find themselves with noses that are too big or chins that are too small. They experience puffy, wrinkled skin; puffy eyes; and drooping jowls—all of which are just as unattractive for them as they are on women.

Most men know that appearance has a direct impact on their careers. *In today's extremely competitive business world and in a growing number of professions, a man wears his resume on his face. Being* qualified isn't always enough anymore, you have to *look* qualified, too.

Worn down, tired-looking executives who appear "over the hill" may get passed over for promotions and raises in favor of younger-looking colleagues. The message comes through loud and clear: the way you look can have a substantial impact on your job and your career. It should come as no surprise, then, that interest in plastic surgery among men has risen sharply over the past decade.

According to the the American Society for Aesthetic Plastic Surgery Inc. and the American Society of Plastic and Reconstructive Surgeons, the following is a list of popular cosmetic surgery options.

Chemical Peel: To restore wrinkled, blemished, unevenly pigmented, or sun-damaged facial skin, the surgeon uses a chemical solution to peel or "strip away" the top layers of the skin. This procedure works best on fair, thin-skinned men who have superficial wrinkles.

Collagen Injections: To plump up creased, furrowed, or sunken facial skin (usually caused by aging or weight loss), collagen (a fatlike substance) is injected into the areas requiring attention. This procedure works best on thin, dry, light-colored skin.

Dermabrasion: To soften sharp edges or surface irregularities including acne and other scars and fine wrinkles around the mouth, the top layers of the skin are mechanically scraped using a high speed rotary wheel.

Blepharoplasty (Eyelid Surgery): To correct drooping upper eyelids and puffy bags below the eyes, this procedure removes excess skin, fat, and muscle. (**Note:** This procedure may be covered by your health insurance if it is used to improve your vision.)

Rhytidectomy (Facelift): To improve sagging facial skin, jowls, and loose neck skin, the surgeon removes excess fat, tightens muscles, and redrapes the skin. This procedure is most often done for men past the age of forty.

Browlift (Forehead lift): To minimize forehead creases, drooping eyes, furrowed forehead and frown lines, excess tissue is removed and the remaining skin is redraped. The procedure is usually requested by men over forty. (**Note:** In this new age of surgical technology, a browlift will definitely not make you a "highbrow.")

Facial Implant: To change the basic shape and balance of the face, a surgeon utilizes carefully styled implants to build up a receding chin, add prominence to cheekbones,

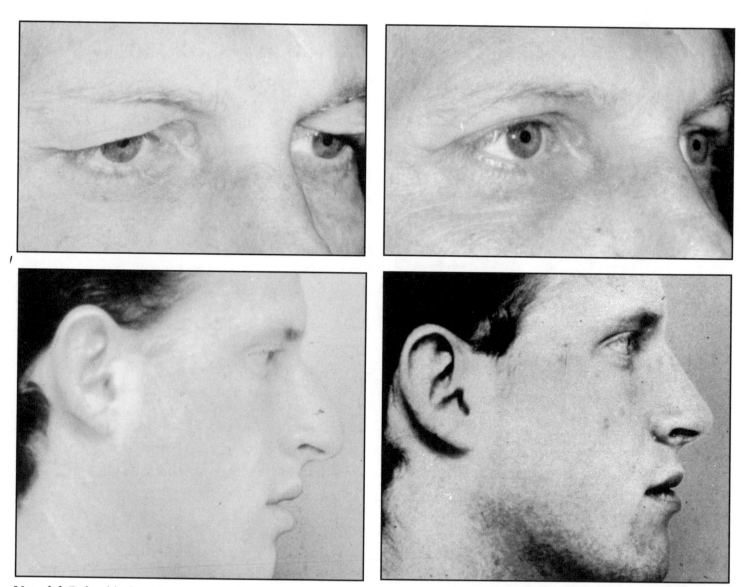

Upper left: Before blepharoplasty. *Upper right*: After the surgery. *Lower left*: Before rhinoplasty. *Lower right*: After the surgery. (Photographs courtesy of The American Society for Aesthetic Plastic Surgery, Inc., Arlington Heights, Illinois)

or to reshape a jawline. (**Note:** Implants may be made of natural or artificial materials.)

Rhinoplasty (Nose Surgery): To reshape the nose by reducing or increasing its size, removing a hump, changing the shape of the tip of the bridge, narrowing the span of the nostrils, or changing the angle between the nose and the upper lip. (**Note:** This procedure may be covered by health insurance if the surgery serves to relieve a breathing problem.)

CHOOSING A PLASTIC SURGEON

It is important to recognize that not every doctor who has claimed the title of plastic surgeon has the same training. According to our experts, anyone with a medical degree can call himself a plastic surgeon. There are no laws that require doctors offering specialty care to meet certain requirements. So if you are considering plastic surgery, check to be sure that any doctor you are considering is certified by the American Board of Plastic Surgery (ABPS). By choosing an ABPS certified surgeon, you can be assured that they have completed at least five years of additional residency training, including three years of surgical training and two years of plastic surgery.

If you are considering surgery for a cosmetic reason, it is advised that you also check to insure that the surgeon is a member of the American Society for Aesthetic Plastic Surgery (ASAPS) or the American Society of Plastic and Reconstructive Surgeons (ASPRS). To locate a qualified plastic surgeon in your area you may call 1–800–635–0625.

If you have a severe problem with scarring, birth marks, burn marks, pitting of the skin from acne or pock marks, or with any of your physical features (nose, eyes, mouth, ears) and it is a source of real anxiety for you, then give serious consideration to having it corrected. Cosmetic surgery is expensive, and most health insurance policies do not cover these procedures. If you feel sure that cosmetic surgery will have a positive effect on your self-confidence and on your life, then don't let your girlfriend, your wife, your family, or anyone talk you out of it. You may hear "I don't care about the way you look, I care about you just the way you are"—and we have no doubt that this comment is made with all sincerity. Just remember, the most important reason for having plastic surgery is so that *you can feel better about yourself*. It's not for anyone else, it's for you.

Utilizing the Image Enhancement Technology offered by aesthetic plastic surgery techniques can raise your Image Quotient 1 to 2 points.

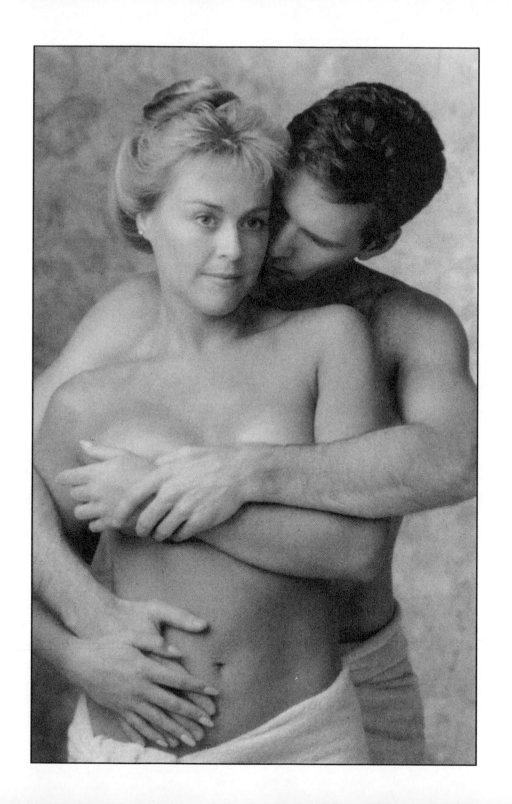

15

Your Sex Life

KEEP IT UP

Normally there are two factors that determine the level of intensity and satisfaction derived from the act of sex. In varying degrees these two factors apply to both men and women. The first concerns your feelings about your partner and what your partner is feeling about you. Feelings of positive emotion toward another individual are encouraged by his or her personal qualities such as kindness, consideration, and intelligence. The second factor in determining the sensitivity and satisfaction of sex is the level of physical attraction you have for your partner and the level of attraction your partner has for you.

It goes without saying that a great many sexual encounters are based almost entirely on physical attraction. All anyone has to do is observe the activity occurring in a singles bar to realize the overpowering effect of purely physical attraction coupled with desire. This attraction is based in large part on the principle we outlined early in our discussion, namely, that we tend to believe that the way people look on the outside is the way they are on the inside. On a nightly basis intelligent men and women still make a very important personal decision based almost exclusively on the way another person looks. The one-night stand can be wildly exciting, but without the development of true emotional feelings, this excitement will not be sustained.

Many men involved in the singles scene begin an evening on the town with great expectations of meeting that special someone with a rating of a 9 or 10. As the night progresses, and after a few cocktails, the standards become lax. It's amazing how all prospective partners seem to get better looking as closing time approaches. Instead of seeking that perfect person who will change your life, maybe you need to take some time to rate yourself. One of the elements of the ideal match is when both partners have essentially compatible intelligence and image quotients. If the old saying "money attracts money" is true, then it is also reasonable to say that an attractive image will entice an attractive image.

A major part of your sex life is governed by your mind; the way you feel about yourself is a vital factor in obtaining ongoing sexual satisfaction. Happiness comes from within and in some cases truly great sex may depend more on the way you feel about yourself than on the physical attributes or beauty of your partner.

It has been established that a man's self-esteem and self-confidence are important factors in his sex life. If you feel good about yourself, this confidence will manifest itself in your sexual performance. But there is one condition that may not always be overcome by improving your image. Many men experience periods of sexual disfunction and have problems obtaining or sustaining an erection, a condition called *impotence*. Less than a decade ago it was believed that most male impotence was the result of psychological problems such as depression or anxiety. Today the reality is that the majority of problems leading to impotence are physical in nature and are caused by abnormalities in blood flow or nerve impulses. If you are experiencing any type of problem in these areas, the good news is that technology now offers a variety of solutions.

The first step is to seek an evaluation from a qualified physician. Your medical history may offer a clue to the source of the problem. For example, some cases of impotence are caused by prescription drugs such as those given for high blood pressure. A physician will be able to determine if the condition is physical or psychological. If the cause of your impotence is psychological, your physician will probably recommend a form of therapy. Visits to a licensed therapist will usually uncover the source of the problem, which have traditionally been stress, anxiety, or depression.

The following is a list of some of the technology now available for those men who are experiencing bouts of impotence resulting from a physical problem.

Hormone Injections: Some men have very low levels of the male hormone testosterone. These low levels can cause temporary or sustained periods of impotence. By injecting *Depo-testosterone* physicians can elevate the testosterone level to a normal range. The only reservation about this procedure is that it could turn off your body's natural production of the hormone thereby making you completely dependent on regular injections. Another possible side effect of testosterone injections is that they bring an added risk of prostate cancer to those men who are classified in a high-risk group.

Penile Injections: For those men who suffer from circulatory problems that inhibit adequate blood flow to the penis, injectable drugs are available that will immediately solve the problem. These circulatory stimulators, such as *phentolamine,* are administered via injection into the lower side of the penis. This treatment results in a full erection in about eight to ten minutes. Penile injections should also be considered for cases of impotence that are not physical in nature, because the stimulation resulting from the injection will usually override any negative messages from the brain.

Implants: When hormone injections or circulatory stimulators fail to produce results, there is always the penile implant. This surgical procedure places a prosthetic device inside the penis. These devices range from semirigid rods to inflatable balloons. Since it is invasive surgery, a penile implant should only be considered when all other options and alternatives have been exhausted.

Along with the fountain of youth, men have been seeking the ultimate aphrodisiac for centuries, that certain something that will maintain levels of passion.

Proper diet, exercise, and rest combine to help insure a robust sex drive. There are many men who believe that ginseng is helpful, and there are others who swear by vitamin E or the mineral zinc. Anthony Chiappone believes that Yohimbine is the most potent stimulator of the male sex drive. Yohimbine is derived from the bark of an African tree and can be purchased in powdered or liquid form at most health food stores. If you want the most powerful version of this product, it is available synthesized and concentrated only by prescription. Yohimbine works because it increases the flow of blood to the penis while decreasing the amount of blood flow from the penis, obviously resulting in a full, firm, lasting erection.

Education is one of the keys to success in this changing world of technology: both the improvement of existing skills and the learning of new skills. We now have a great deal of information available on enhancing the pleasures of sex. There is much to learn that our parents did not know. It has been said that "know-how is the best aphrodisiac" and that there is no such thing as a "born lover." Two of America's top sex educators, Dr. Derek C. Polonsky of the Harvard Medical School and certified sex therapist Dr. Marian E. Dunn, have compiled a complete catalog of intimate lovemaking positions. This information is available on an educational videotape titled "Sexual Positions for Lovers." This videotape provides exciting and reassuring information, giving the viewer an excellent foundation for understanding how various positions will stimulate different parts of the body. It is available through the Sinclair Video Library in Chapel Hill, North Carolina. The explicit nature of this tape will provide you with the most current information regarding intimacy-building skills and techniques for more enjoyable foreplay and intercourse.

We have detailed some surgical and nonsurgical solutions to problems regarding sexual disfunction. For most men the real secret to a fulfilled sex life begins with personal self-esteem, which is based largely on a positive self-image.

16

Makeup for Men

MEN AND MAKEUP

Many of you still have vivid memories of going to the barber shop every other Saturday morning with your father. For younger readers, barber shops were usually small storefront businesses with a peppermint (red, white, and blue) pole out in front. Barber shops were places for men only, not to be confused with the elaborate salons we visit today. A haircut in the 1940s took about five minutes, unless you and the barber became engrossed in discussing some topic of the day. At the conclusion of this brief clipping procedure, the barber would splash on some scented hair tonic to plaster down those wild clipped ends of hair. Many men would decline this final step because they did not want to "smell like a sissy." Today, it is hard to believe that that lucrative industry currently marketing various men's fragrances came into existence and flourished only during the past fifty years or so.

For all our claims to the contrary, the impact advertising has on our everyday lives is extraordinary. Going back about forty years, the sales of hair coloring to women were virtually nonexistent. Of course women colored their hair but the prevailing opinion was that only "hussies" or wanton women would ever change the natural color of their hair. The Clairol Company broke through this well-entrenched attitude with a massive ad campaign, asking the double-edged question: "Does she or doesn't she?" Today, the sale of hair coloring to both women and men is a billion-dollar-a-year business.

In the early part of this book we outlined the changing role of males in our society and that the main reason for this change rested with advances in technology. It does not indicate any reduction in the importance or pleasures of manhood: on the contrary, men should now live longer, happier, more successful lives. Men are now incorporating into their lives many and varied techniques for changing how they look to others and how they are perceived in life situations. Men diet to lose weight, exercise to firm up, have their hair cut to suit the times, choose clothes that complement their physiques and their personal tastes, and use a large number of personal and hygiene products to become more appealing to others. The history of male image in the United States illustrates that men initially rejected a great many products that today are considered common place. Activities and the use of image-enhancing products and services that were viewed as the sole province of women gradually became accepted in modern male circles. One need only consider the following short list of examples to see how far men have come in implementing Image Enhancement Technology.

- The use of hair colors, rinses, and bleaches

- The use of deodorants and antiperspirants

- The use of colognes

- The use of hairspray, mousses, gels

- The acceptance of unisex hair salons

- The use of hair dryers

- The use of moisturizing and antiwrinkle creams

- The wearing of jewelry (pierced earrings and necklaces)

The list could be extended but you see what we mean. Men have changed the way they view the use of many products and services. The idea of men wearing makeup to enhance their facial features is a logical next step in the evolution of the male image.

AS NATURE INTENDED

It is interesting to note how our culture and subsequent buying habits have been changed within the past half century. An example of this change is shown by the statistics relative to the sale of deodorants. Prior to the Second World War less than 20 percent of the American public used a deodorant on a regular basis. Of this 20 percent the majority were women. Now a vast array of deodorants and antiperspirants specifically targeted to men clog the shelves of supermarkets and drugstores. Every passing year brings change to our culture and the things we find acceptable, and even deem necessary. Sometimes these changes occur so slowly we are not aware of their magnitude and how they have affected our thinking, our personal habits, and our lives in general. In the very near future, it is possible that a man's makeup kit will be placed alongside his shaving kit in the bathroom cabinet.

Men are currently spending a fortune on products they hope will make them look better. Some of these products are of little or no value. Obviously, the man who really takes care of himself, utilizing the latest technologies relating to diet and exercise, will look better than the man with a self-destructive lifestyle. But one glaring fact remains: You can work out, eat all the right foods, and can get your body in tip-top shape, but your face may still not project your desired image. There may be darkness and lines under your eyes, your face may look puffy or drawn, you may be noticing unwanted wrinkles or crow's-feet. Too many days in the sun or too many years on the calendar can take their toll. We have shared with you some of the surgical solutions to facial transformation, but if you feel you do not require anything quite so drastic yet still want to look your best, then the answer may be *makeup.*

Many men, and even some women, say they will never use makeup because they want to live their lives "as nature intended." This statement may appear very noble on the surface, but it is really an unfortunate self-deception. If you give some thought to this, you must agree that virtually every aspect of your life is enhanced by products that are not created by "nature." The following is a checklist of some *unnatural* things that must be eliminated by anyone who is really determined to live life purely as nature intended. If you hold to such a view, you would not be able to use:

soap
an automobile
any electrical appliances
airplanes
gas or electric heat
air conditioning
antibiotics
surgical procedures
toothpaste
deodorant
razors, etc.

This list could be extended quite a bit, but you see what we mean. No doubt some of you will say that the comparison of men using makeup to using a deodorant is absurd. But don't forget, it's only been a few decades since men accepted the use of deodorants. The objection doesn't seem to hold up.

Nature has given us the intellect and the raw materials to achieve greater comfort and happiness in our lives. *Any product that can enrich our lives is "as nature intended."*

HISTORICAL FACTS ABOUT MEN AND MAKEUP

In various respected professions, men wearing makeup is considered acceptable and in fact necessary. People who work in the theater, in television, and in motion pictures have used makeup to present a more natural look under harsh lighting conditions. The fact is men have worn makeup since the dawn of recorded time. Through many archaeological finds and extensive research, experts have learned that cosmetics have been in existence long before religion.

Developed by men, cosmetics were used to elevate a man's physical and spiritual presence. Men were the first to wear cosmetics, and continued to do so for more than ten thousand years. Archaeologists in Egypt have uncovered eye paint ground from green malachite and black antimony powder, used to shape eyebrows much like the familiar eyebrow pencil used today. Based on drawings and other information, it was found that both of these forms of makeup were used exclusively by men. The Egyptian men would use the black powder on their eyelids, extending it as far as their temples, to create the "wing effect" we see pictured on the walls of their ancient tombs dating back to 5000 B.C.E. The green malachite that was used as the base for the eye paint became for Egypt a major item of trade with other countries. Makeup itself became a major export item for the merchants of Egypt.

Around 3500 B.C.E. the Egyptian art of makeup for men had progressed to the point that their range of eye shadows extended from blue to purple. Egyptians of status began coloring their cheeks and their mouths. Since the use of makeup was restricted to men of the upper class it became a symbol of the elite. It was not uncommon for the Egyptian nobleman to display his personal collection of makeup in gold containers in some prominent place in his home. In the tomb of King Tutankhamen, rated by archaeologists as one of the best sources of information on the lifestyle and products of its era, was found the world's first sophisticated line of cosmetics.

By 2000 B.C.E. the Assyrians had surpassed the Egyptians in the art of personal display. Along with ornate dress, the upper-class use of makeup had become the standard among all kings and nobles. The Persians imitated this style of dress and makeup, which ultimately spread to the Roman Empire and the royal courts of Europe.

In the writings of Vatsayana, the author and compiler of the Kama Sutra, the classic Hindu treatise on love and sexual conduct, he encouraged the elite merchant class to experiment with cosmetics and perfumes, as well as a variety of sexual pleasures.

In other parts of the world native tribesmen protected themselves against what they believed to be forces of evil by painting very complex designs on their faces thereby creating an image of immortality. It is interesting to note that men were the first to paint their faces for protective purposes because they were the first to leave the compound to hunt for food, gather supplies, and defend against tribal enemies.

The elaborate designs that the tribesmen painted on their faces were known as devil masks. It was believed that a man who knew how to paint himself a powerful devil mask would be protected from harm by enemies. Certain tribes were known to favor specific designs, so the face paint gave the tribesmen a sense of identity. Depending on the situation, the ability to change their disguise was strategically beneficial, as warriors painted on new and different designs to confuse their enemies.

The ancient art of tattooing is one primitive custom involving men's cosmetics that has survived to this day. This unique practice of puncturing the skin with a needle and then injecting a dye to create a permanent design was developed by the Egyptians around 3000 B.C.E. About two thousand years later the art of tattooing was brought to Japan by the Ainu, a migrant tribe who developed tattooing into a religious ritual. Along with the Maori, a tribe in New Zealand, the Japanese perfected the elaborate use of color and form.

Europeans were introduced to tattooing in 1691 by seaman William Dampier. Hoping to cash in on a curiosity, Dampier brought a tattooed man from the South Sea Islands to the London sideshow stages. He billed the native as "Omai, The

Painted Prince." During one of his voyages to Tahiti, Captain James Cook witnessed the art of tattooing and found it intriguing. Cook described the tattoos as "beautiful circles, crescent and ornamental." To sailors, the tattoo was believed to be a good luck charm portraying an image of masculinity and adventure.

The tattoo is more popular today than at any time in history and its acceptance crosses most economic, social, and even sexual barriers. Tattooing is now used in cosmetic medicine to remove unwanted birthmarks by injecting them with a pigment the color of the natural skin. In modern society a tattoo is no longer reserved for the free-spirited motorcycle rider: they can be found on the hips, shoulders, and ankles of men and women at beaches around the world. This primitive form of men's cosmetics is now a mark of high fashion, whether it be a look of permanent eyeliner applied by a licensed professional or just a temporary cosmetic tattoo that can be washed off the next day.

By the fifteenth century many men in the royal courts of Europe used makeup, while the majority of women of status still were reluctant to do so. Even the most masculine knights of the court used skin rouge and powder. During the eighteenth century, the king of France, Louis XIV, was determined to outdo his cousin Charles II of England. The French king established a standard that brought the use of men's makeup to new heights. From his court came a man whose name, even today, is synonymous with the dapper male image—Beau Brummell.

We all know the song "Yankee Doodle," but until we conducted research for this book, we never knew what was meant by the line: "He stuck a feather in his hat and called it Macaroni." In the 1770s a group of displaced Europeans, known as the Macaronis, came to America. The men of this group mimicked the dress and customs (including the use of makeup) of European royalty. Their flamboyant wardrobes and attention to their appearance was viewed with great disdain among the Christian, Puritan, working-class Americans. In the eyes of the Puritans, the Macaronis "were seducers contrary to moral values."

The curtailment of the use of makeup by men actually happened as a result of the demise of royalty and the emergence of more democratic and socialistic types of government, which eliminated many of the traditions of the so-called privileged classes, and replaced them with the values and practices of the farmers and the working-class people.

It was not until the early 1900s that women began using makeup to any great degree. Prior to that time our Puritan background held to the belief that any woman who would "paint her face" must be of loose virtue. Even with today's depressed economic conditions, the average man lives better and has more creature comforts than the royalty of yesteryear. The man of today is realizing that, to meet and beat the competition, every aspect of his emotional, intellectual, and physical persona must be maximized. Makeup offers a perfect tool to help achieve this overall objective.

THE MIRACLE OF MAKEUP

Many years ago, a friend of Richard named Ed was married to Nora, one of the most gorgeous women Richard had ever seen. On many occasions Richard and one of his dates would join Ed and Nora for an evening on the town. It was often a little disturbing to Richard since none of his dates ever seemed to come close to Ed's wife in the glamour department. She was the kind of woman you talk about when you say "she turned every head in the room." Nora was a knockout and very classy; she really had it all—the face, the figure, and the personality. Ed had a rather short temper, and on more than one occasion became involved in physical altercations with men who would stare at Nora or try to strike up a conversation with her. Her beauty was always the center of attention at a party, in a restaurant, or even in a department store.

One Saturday night, after an evening on the town, Richard and his date stopped at Ed's house for coffee before they headed for home. The next day Richard's date called him to say that she had left her jacket at Ed's house: she requested that Richard pick it up for her. Since it would just take a minute to pick up the jacket, Richard did not bother to call to say he was coming over.

When Richard arrived at the house that Sunday morning he rang the front doorbell and was greeted by a stranger. Richard knew Ed had a sister (though he had never met her) so he thought nothing more about the stranger. The woman let Richard into the house as he began to explain how he visited Ed and Nora last night and that his date had left her jacket. Without answering, the woman turned toward the staircase and shouted for Ed. As Ed appeared on the stairs, she turned abruptly and walked into another room. As Ed approached Richard, he began to laugh nervously, "Boy, will she be angry at me." "Who was that lady?" Richard asked. Now Ed really began to laugh. "That was no lady; that was Nora. Boy, is she going to be mad. When the doorbell rang she wanted me to answer it, but I assured her it was just the newsboy. Instead, you show up. She does look a little different when she's not all fixed up, doesn't she?"

A "little different" was the understatement of the century. It was impossible to believe that it had really been Nora. There was virtually nothing attractive about the woman who answered the door that morning. When we met again the following weekend, Nora excused herself for being so rude, but went on to explain that she did not like seeing people when she wasn't prepared.

The fact was that Nora's looks were only average, but she had mastered the art of applying makeup. We don't mean the big false eyelashes, the heavy rouge, and the lipstick that showgirls wear. Nora had mastered the art of camouflaging all her weak points and creating an incredible vision of beauty. The great figure was there, the great personality was there, but it all would have gone practically unnoticed if it were not for those five or six items she carried in the little cosmetic bag in her purse.

It has been almost thirty years since that Sunday morning. Some readers might think that Nora was living a lie because she needed makeup to face the world. Surely this must be the height of insecurity. But let's look at Nora's created image another way. Because of the way she looked she met and married Ed, a very successful building contractor and home developer. As of this writing, Ed and Nora (not their real names) have been happily married for more than thirty-two years. After their children entered college, Nora took her great image to the job market, and went on to become one of the top real-estate salespersons in upstate New York. She has won numerous sales awards, and is still making an excellent living. She remains a vision of beauty.

Nora is an extremely intelligent and warm human being who always combined diet and exercise to develop and maintain that great figure. But she knew that if she wanted to get the most out of life, she had to look her very best. She utilized the miracle of makeup in attaining a level of personal and professional success that most people could only dream about.

Makeup was originally developed by men for men. Today's man can gain the many advantages offered by utilizing the advanced technology of men's makeup.

THE NEW MALE GROOMING STANDARD

One of the major complaints registered by the feminist movement is that women are viewed in our culture as sex objects. Many beauty pageants have been boycotted and picketed to protest this physical emphasis on womanhood. A secondary message is that society rates a man based solely on his intellect and achievements and that his appearance is not a factor. Incredible as it may seem, many men really believe this is true.

The hardcore feminist becomes very upset when we show that she often uses the same criteria to rate men as men do to rate women. The admiration for and magnetic attraction of an appealing physical image is not a masculine trait; it is a *human trait*.

Despite the objections of the feminists, women wisely continue to spend billions of dollars annually for personal grooming and cosmetic items for their skin, hair, and nails, not to mention the additional money spent to achieve weight loss. And during the past couple of decades men have become aware of the importance of creating and maintaining their personal image.

Of the tens of thousands of "how to" books on the market, we can unequivocally state that *For Men Only* is unlike any other ever written. It will officially mark the beginning of a new revolution in male image enhancement, namely, men's cosmetic makeup, a phenomenon that will set a new masculine grooming standard before the end of this decade. Included in the total concept of Image Enhancement Technology is information on men's makeup and how it will personally benefit you in both your career and your personal life. Most importantly, we will now provide you with step-by-step instructions on how you can transform your image through the use of makeup.

ARE MEN ACCEPTING THE CHALLENGE?

As Dorian Cosmetics International reaches its tenth year, we have established a customer base of over twenty thousand. Like any other business, successful marketing required that we know more about our customers. To solicit this information, we have been sending questionnaires to those who ordered products over the years. We offered a small gift for their prompt response. The questions solicited the respondent's age, marital status, and occupation. Here are some of the important demographics we learned from a 37 percent response to this customer survey:

36 percent were married,
28 percent were over age fifty,
68 percent were professionals,
76 percent were involved in a fitness program.

Also uncovered in our survey was the fact that we could count a state supreme court judge, several physicians, two nationally known bodybuilders, and an NFL placekicker among our customers. We also found we had customers involved in law enforcement and in all branches of the military.

There is one major issue that we must address before offering a detailed discussion of makeup for men. Until quite recently, the idea of men wearing makeup may have been associated with the user's sexual orientation. Not unlike the initial macho male response to the use of hair sprays, hair dryers, deodorants, and colognes by men, some will insist that only effeminate or homosexual males would buy and use male makeup. Our assessment of the Dorian Cosmetics' clientele does not support this view. For many years all our advertising has been in the pages of *Exercise for Men* and *Natural Bodybuilding* magazines. Based on the readership of these two publications and our survey, it appears that the majority of our customers are heterosexual. We believe it more probable that you will find a Dorian customer at a country club dance with his wife or girlfriend or at a ladies' night in some singles bar. Don't forget that a significant number of our clients were and are women who purchase these products for their husbands or boyfriends. Using men's makeup has nothing to do with sexual orientation. It has everything to do with making you look better to compete and succeed in today's world and the world of tomorrow.

A FEW TESTIMONIALS

Over the past ten years we have received many letters from our customers, letters telling of personal experience, and how the use of our products has enhanced not only their appearance but their lives. The following are excerpts from just a few.

"I have been searching for a men's cosmetic line for years. I have chemical burn scars that I got from combat service in Vietnam. Usually the scars are not bad, but sometimes they do get very red. When these scars flare up, I used to get very self-conscience and tried to stay out of everyone's way. Since using your products I don't have any more of these bad days."

R.S.

Hays, Kansas

"I am a twenty-four-year-old customer. I live in West Virginia. . . . I have fair skin and in the winter I used to look real pale. My skin is dry and oily at the same time, if that makes any sense.

"Until I sent for your products, all I could do was wait for summer. The sun was the only thing that helped my skin. Now I look good twelve months a year, and my skin feels a lot better."

G.L.

W. Virginia

"I had acne when I was a youngster and the scars are still there. Your Camouflage/ Concealer has solved a problem that I have had for more than fifteen years. I also use it on my upper back when I have my shirt off in the summer."

D.L.

Baltimore, Maryland

"I am very thankful there is finally a product that suits medium complected black males. I am very fussy about my appearance when I go out in public. Your products are amazing."

J.T.

Oakland, California

"I have a condition referred to as Albino. I have good features, but have very little color in my skin, eyes, or hair. Believe me when I tell you, your products have changed my life. Your company should be designated as a public service organization."

K.F.

New York, New York

MAKEUP: THE BASIC PRINCIPLES

The question that you may be asking at this point is, what is the difference between makeup for men and that used by women? There are several significant differences. First, in general, a woman's pores are smaller than a man's, therefore the cosmetic formulations used in men's cosmetics must be of thicker consistency to provide smooth, even coverage. Only natural "earth tones" are used in men's cosmetics as opposed to the multitude of vivid colors found in women's makeup. There are no products for the lips or the eyelids since these areas accentuate feminine features. Ask your wife or girlfriend to apply her makeup but not to use any lipstick or eye shadow. Notice the significant difference this change in makeup application produces. The word "handsome" is used to describe a man's good looks, while "beautiful" or "pretty" is used to describe an attractive woman. Men's cosmetics are designed to make you look handsome.

Most men reading this book will have never applied makeup of any kind. This section will give you a crash course on how makeup is applied using a minimum of effort while gaining the maximum effect. Those of you who have seen a magician perform or who practice magic as a hobby are familiar with the term "misdirection," which describes the way the magician draws the audience's attention to something he wants them to see so that he can do something else that he does not want them to see. A similar approach is taken when makeup is applied. If you are like most people, you have both strong and weak points in your facial structure. One of the most effective uses of makeup is to accent your strong features making them dominate your image, while softening your weak points. Makeup is not a mask, but it will serve to greatly enhance your natural appearance.

Facial Structure

Before we proceed with the instructions for applying makeup you should determine what kind of facial structure you have. There are four basic face shapes: oval, round, square, and long. If you need help visualizing the basic facial structures, refer to chapter 12 in which each common shape is discussed relative to choosing eyewear.

The best way to determine your face shape is to study your face in a mirror. According to art books that deal with drawing the human face and form, the ideal feminine face is oval while the ideal masculine face tends to be more square. With a minimum of practice you can create a very strong, handsome, masculine image. The application of makeup creates an optical illusion that accentuates your best features while deemphasizing other aspects of your face. The basic rule in applying makeup is to darken the areas you wish to play down while lightening those areas you wish to emphasize.

The time spent putting on your makeup will probably be about the same as that spent on your morning shave. The use of makeup will require a few more minutes in your personal grooming regime, but its benefits will be worth the extra time you spend. Makeup for men will never include the number of products available for women. The new Dorian makeup kit for men has only four items:

(1) Camouflage Foundation/Concealer
(2) Transforming (Bronzer) Base
(3) Structural Enhancer
(4) MascuLINE Pencil and MANscara

The Dorian makeup kit.

There are five versions of the Dorian kit to accommodate all basic skin types—Caucasian, African American, Asian, Latin American, and Mediterranean—but the simple application steps are the same for all skin types.

Since the "light of day" shows much more color, makeup should be applied more conservatively for the daylight hours. When it is done correctly it should be completely undetectable. In the evening, you can be more liberal since artificial light tends to drain and blend colors.

When you first begin to use makeup you will probably stop at every mirror to check how you look. I remember one evening when we demonstrated our products to a prominent attorney; he kept looking in every glass that reflected his face. Later that evening, in a restaurant, while looking at himself in a mirror, he actually walked into a wall. No words can fully describe the incredible changes you can bring about by using these makeup products. Once you have personally experienced the benefits makeup has to offer, you will quickly realize the positive difference it can make in your life.

Preparation

Keep in mind that the intent of using makeup is to optimize your image. To achieve that end you need a well-prepared foundation. Before applying makeup at the beginning of the day, and at the end of the day after using makeup, it is vital that you wash your face thoroughly. Oddly enough, you probably have better skin than most of the women you know. Because men shave every morning we are removing dead skin cells from our faces. This has the effect of renewing our skin tone. Since women don't shave their faces, they must use special cleansing products to remove the dead skin cells that we scrape off every morning.

Though shaving does help you in preparing your face for applying makeup, we recommend buying a soap made specifically for your skin type: dry, oily, or normal. Most people have "combination skin": some parts of the face are oily while other parts are dry. The skin tends to be dry around the eyes because there are no oil glands in this area of the face. The skin is usually oily in the T Zone (the T-shaped area extending across the middle of your forehead, down your nose and toward your chin). This is the portion of your face where oil glands are most active. Since the Dorian Transforming Base is also a moisturizer, we suggest the use of a soap made for oily skin. The soap will remove the excess oil while the moisturizer will replace the oils lost in the dry areas.

Cleansing

Washing your face, either in the shower or at the bathroom sink, should not involve stretching or pulling the skin. Don't use your washcloth as if you were cleaning your tires; vigorous harsh rubbing action that tends to move the skin on your face will cause damage by diminishing the skin's elasticity (its flexibility). These movements, especially as you get older, can cause a sagging appearance to the face. After using soap, we suggest the use of an exfoliating scrub to remove the imbedded dirt and any remaining dead skin cells without damaging the skin.

The temperature of the water used to cleanse your face should be only as warm as needed. Water that is too hot will tend to open your pores and relax the muscles of the face and may contribute to a more flaccid appearance. It is a good idea to rinse your face with cold water: this closes your pores and gives your face a tighter, more youthful appearance. Failure to close your pores after a hot shower or bath can contribute to pimples and skin eruptions because the skin is open to invasion by bacteria.

Toning

For healthy, fresh, firm skin, your pores need to be closed. To achieve this toned look, you can just use cold water or make up your own mixture of equal parts apple cider vinegar and cold water. This mixture offers an advantage because, after it dries, it tends to normalize the pH balance of the skin. The term pH refers to a chemical measurement scale of the balance between acids and alkalines on the skin's surface.

If you had a bad night, you can rejuvenate your facial skin tone to correct the appearance of puffy or baggy eyes with the use of an ice pack. Place the ice pack over your face for ten minutes, then rinse with lukewarm water followed by cold water. This simple procedure will tighten your pores and generate a healthy, well-rested appearance. We recommend this procedure only for occasional use. As we have pointed out, there is no substitute for getting adequate rest.

The Dorian Method in Four Steps

Keep these observations in mind when applying makeup. First, avoid overhead lighting: it creates shadows on your face, especially under your eyes. This creates a problem in attaining a natural look. Lighting positioned on both sides of the face is most desirable. Second, whenever possible apply makeup in the same type of lighting in which you'll be seen. Most clothing stores have removed fluorescent lighting because its reflection can create a false sense of color. This is also true of skin coloring. If you are going out for the day, try to apply your makeup in natural daylight. Third, if you wear contact lenses, remember to put them on *before* applying makeup. Not only will you be able to see what you're doing, but you won't risk wrecking your fine job by stretching or pulling your skin to insert the lenses.

Step 1: The Camouflage/Concealer

This product was originally developed by cosmetologists as a corrective measure to conceal birthmarks, scars, and burns. The Camouflage/Concealer blends in without being detected yet it hides such problem areas as discoloration, broken capillaries, and darkness under the eyes. Most men have absolutely no idea what an extraordinary improvement is achieved just by making the skin an even color.

Before makeup is applied, men may encounter such problems as wrinkles, laugh lines, lines and circles under the eyes, skin discoloration, and blemishes.

After Step #1: Camouflage Concealer, the dark circles and lines under the eyes are radically softened or eliminated, the blemishes are covered, and areas of discoloration are no longer apparent. (Illustrations courtesy of Heather Harvey and Shirley Lombardo)

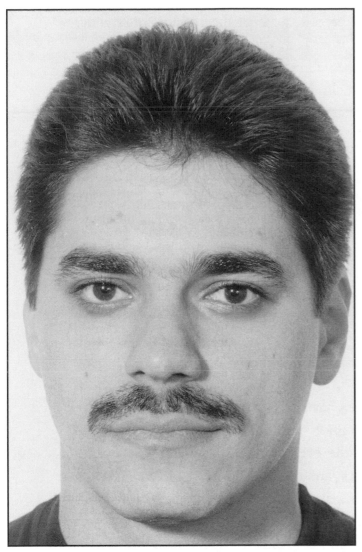 

Before   STEP #1   After

The visual elimination of dark circles under your eyes will make you look younger; the covering of blemishes, broken capillaries, and areas of discoloration will enhance your appearance dramatically. (Photographs © Frank M. Luterek)

A reddish nose, forehead, or chin can seriously detract from your overall appearance. An area of discoloration on your face can become a visual focal point, nullifying everything else you do with your wardrobe, your hair, your teeth, and the like.

The use of Camouflage/Concealer alone will create a significant improvement in the appearance of many men. The visual elimination of dark circles under your eyes can make you look younger. The visual elimination of blemishes, broken capillaries, and areas of facial discoloration will make you appear better looking.

To apply Camouflage/Concealer, use your index finger to place "dots" of the makeup to all areas that need attention, such as red blotches, blemishes, broken capillaries, dark areas (under the eyes), shaving nicks and/or minor scars, and so on.

Now, using a circular motion, blend the dots evenly and smoothly to completely cover all problem areas. There is a specific color tone of Camouflage/Concealer to match your skin type so when you have completely blended each area there should be no points where the areas with Camouflage/Concealer and those without are noticeable.

Do you see the improvement in your appearance after applying only this first step?

A *note about corrective makeup*: Many men have facial imperfections: birthmarks, minor scars, patches of discoloration, and minor burn marks. There are also other conditions such as heavy darkness under the eyes or reddish skin on the nose. Any of these problems can be a source of anxiety that leads to a loss of self-confidence. There are many recorded cases in which severe scars or burns on the face result in antisocial or even reclusive behavior. The application of Camouflage/Concealer will visually correct most of these common imperfections. Those unsightly birthmarks, scars, burns, dark circles, and the like can be eliminated in a matter of minutes.

You may now proceed immediately to Step #2.

Before   After

Applying makeup will correct many facial imperfections: birthmarks, pockmarks, minor scars, patches of discoloration, and burn marks, among others. (Photographs © Frank M. Luterek)

Step #2: Transforming (Bronzer) Base

Next you will apply the Transforming (Bronzer) Base, a product that will have the visual effect of giving you a new skin. There are three types of bases to accommodate the various human pigmentations: light, medium, and deep. These products are designed to bring the tone and color of a man's skin to a widely accepted standard.

If you are fair complexioned you'll use the deep base. This will provide you with that healthy, bronzed "outdoor" look. African-American men with very dark complexions often order the light base, bringing them toward what they consider to be the accepted ideal. Along with providing color and tone, the Transforming (Bronzer) Base is also a moisturizer and a sunscreen (SPF 8). As pointed out in the skin-care section, contrary to popular belief, moisturizers are not effective in *bringing moisture into the skin*; rather they act to *seal in the existing body moisture*. Ironically, women spend a fortune on moisturizing creams when they could save a great deal of money by using a little petroleum jelly, which would do the job better.

The amount of moisture in your skin is the major factor in the appearance of aging. Remember, the only difference between a grape and a raisin is moisture. The use of Transforming (Bronzer) Base not only provides an immediate cosmetic improvement, it is a treatment for your skin along with protection from the adverse effects of the sun.

There used to be a popular saying about the various choices we make: "Everything is a tradeoff." If we want one thing, we have to give up another. Well, if you insist on lying in the sun for hours to acquire a tan, you assume the risks connected with that choice. Now with Image Enhancement Technology, you can have the benefit of a golden tan while at the same time doing something good for your skin.

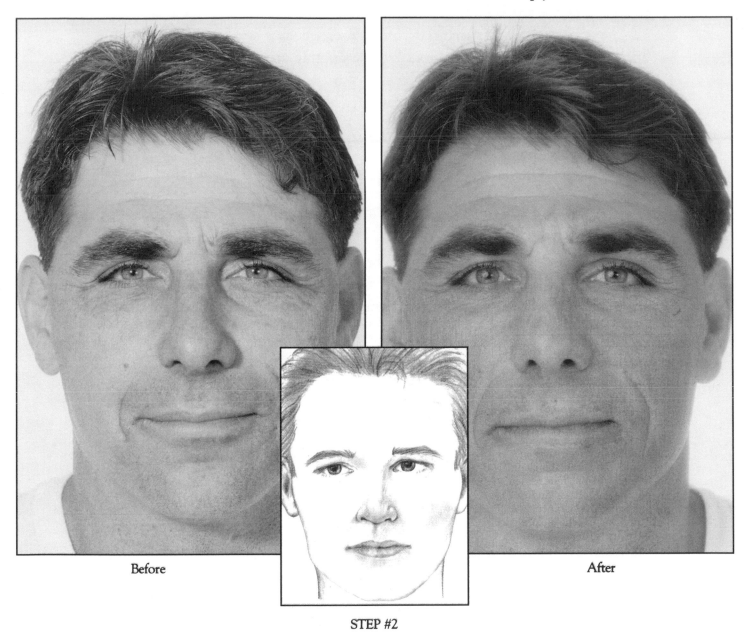

Before

STEP #2

After

After applying Transforming (Bronzer) Base, the face has a healthy look, almost like new skin. Any remaining lines or wrinkles are further softened or eliminated. (Illustration courtesy of Heather Harvey and Shirley Lombardo; photographs © Frank M. Luterek)

To apply the Transforming (Bronzer) Base, squeeze a small amount onto your fingertips. Using a circular motion, blend smoothly and evenly over your entire face. You may wish to consider the use of a cosmetic sponge to complete this procedure. It will help insure even consistency. Make sure to apply the bronzer to all areas of your face right up to your hairline. There should be no lines of demarcation where the ending point of the bronzer application is visually obvious in contrast to your natural skin color. Pay special attention to your jawline, your neck, and your ears to ensure even coverage.

Now use a facial tissue and lightly wipe away any excess bronzer from your cheeks, nose, and forehead. Be sure there is no excess bronzer around your neck and jawline; it can soil shirt collars. The bronzer is resistant to streaking or running: you can wear it everyday for all activities from the health club to the night club.

Now stand back and look at the man looking at you through the mirror. Yes, it is amazing. Proceed now to Step #3.

Step #3: The Structural Enhancer

Look in the mirror and consider the shape of your face. The objective of this product is to highlight your bone structure and create your ideal masculine appearance. The geometric shape of the square consists of four lines of equal length intersecting at 90 degree angles. Obviously, no man's face is really square but the perceived ideal male face has a visual appearance of tending toward this design. In the romance novels the hero is often described as having a square jaw and square temples.

To apply Structural Enhancer (these instructions pertain to all facial shapes), locate your cheekbone; it is the fullest part of your cheek. Following the line of your cheekbone, apply Enhancer using upward and outward strokes toward your ear. Use your ear as a guide when applying Enhancer to your cheekbones: do not apply the product on areas of the face higher than the top of your ear or lower than the ear lobes. Use a facial tissue or a cotton ball to blend it in until you achieve a completely natural look.

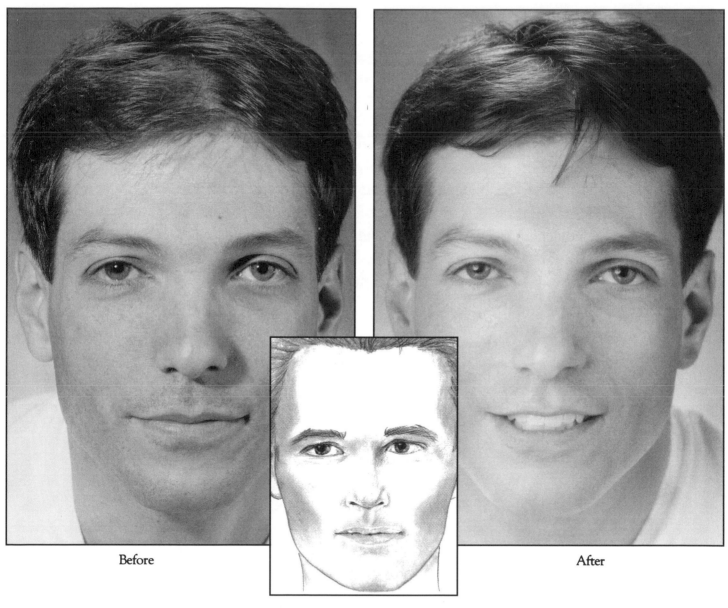

Before

STEP #3

After

With the application of Structural Enhancer your face has just changed shape, reflecting the more square, masculine ideal. (Illustration courtesy of Heather Harvey and Shirley Lombardo; photographs © Frank M. Luterek)

Note: If your face is thin and your cheeks tend to be hollow (sunken), use Structural Enhancer very sparingly because it will make your face look even thinner.

If your face is more round, apply some extra Transforming (Bronzer) Base just below your cheekbones. This serves as a contour shadow that darkens your cheeks. Since darkness will be perceived as visually reducing the size of your jaw, the shadow will give your face a more angled look. (In other words, the Bronzer will help to square your jaw.) Next apply some extra deep Transforming Bronzer Base along the jawline, under the chin, and at the temples: this will create a slimming effect. The combined use of Structural Enhancer (which gives your cheekbones more prominence) and deep Transforming (Bronzer) Base (which darkens or shades your face) can have a dramatic effect in producing a more ideal masculine appearance.

Look in the mirror: your image has just changed shape. Now you can proceed to Step #4.

Step #4: MascuLINE Pencil and MANscara

Every man can improve his appearance by applying Camouflage Concealer, Transforming (Bronzer) Base, and Structural Enhancer. As demonstrated by most successful male models and media personalities, the discrete use of cosmetics for the eyes can make a positive difference. Generally speaking, only a select group consisting of those men whose eyes may appear dull due to lack of pigmentation or a lack of color or fullness in their eyelashes need to master Step #4. Many women still do not know how to use cosmetics on their eyes, and any man who chooses to use the eye pencil and/or MANscara must exercise *discretion* to create a natural appearance. Remember, the best makeup does not appear obvious.

More than any other facial feature, your eyes give expression to your face. Your eyes can communicate fear or courage, hate or love, trust or suspicion, health or illness, interest or boredom. In several surveys, women have named a man's eyes as being his most attractive attribute. We have all heard expressions such as "He has cold eyes," "He has sneaky eyes," "He has this blank stare." Have

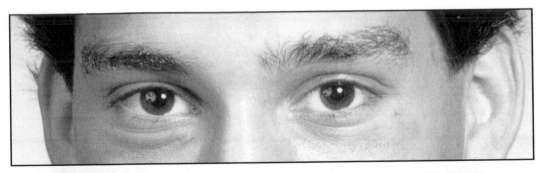

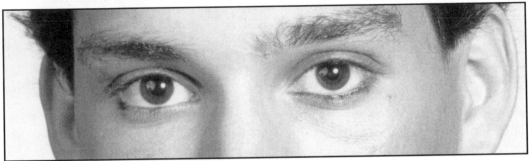

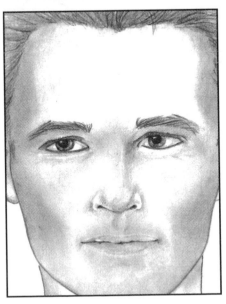

Top: Before applying MascuLINE Pencil MANscara. *Middle and bottom*: After the application. For those who want to add definition to their eyes, this part of the makeup kit can prove invaluable. (Illustration courtesy of Heather Harvey and Shirley Lombardo; photographs © Paul Petock)

you ever seen the stare down that often takes place between two opponents in a boxing match? Each boxer looks directly into the other's eyes. This is done for two reasons: first to communicate hostility toward the opponent and second to look for signs of fear. Every man wants to appear confident and in control. Your eyes can send this message. Remember, the purpose of men's eye makeup is to *accent* your eyes not to *accentuate* them.

To apply MascuLINE Pencil, remember that it is always a good idea to keep your pencil sharpened. You might want to put your pencil in the freezer the night before sharpening it: freezing hardens the eyelining material, which creates a more precise point when sharpened. Now, begin at the inside corner of the lower eyelid and gently trace the natural line of the eye to the outside corner. Using your index finger, gently fade in (slightly erase) the line you have just made. This insures an undetectable yet meaningful effect. Do not use MascuLINE Pencil on your upper eyelids, because it tends to overpower the desired effect of creating a subtle accent.

To apply MANscara, be sure it is the right type for your hair color. (For best results stipulate your hair color when ordering.) Remove the applicator brush from the tube and discreetly brush MANscara to your upper and lower eyelashes. (Apply the product only to the *top side* of the *upper* lashes, and to the *bottom side* of the *lower* lashes. Applying to both sides of upper and lower lashes will overpower the desired effect.) While applying MANscara to the *upper* eyelashes, use an upward motion of the wrist, going from the base to the tip of your lashes. While applying MANscara to the *lower* eyelashes, use a downward motion of the wrist, going from the base to the tip of your lashes. Check to make sure you have maintained a natural look after applying MANscara. After the application, we suggest using a child's toothbrush to remove any excess and to seperate each individual hair in each set of lashes.

If you want to know how eye makeup, discreetly applied, can enhance your appearance, just look at many network news anchormen, major talk show hosts, and even national politicians.

Now stand back and look at yourself in the mirror. What you have accomplished

This dramatic transformation of coauthor Richard Derwald is the result of the Image Enhancement Technologies of hair color, hair replacement, and the four steps of makeup for men. (Photographs © Frank M. Luterek)

represents the ultimate in cosmetic Image Enhancement Technology. The Dorian four-step makeup application procedure can produce a final result that should transform your appearance and positively affect your life.

Your Image Quotient has now been improved by at least 1 to 2 points.

In Summary

The ability to apply makeup is a learned skill. It requires practice and a little experimenting to create the image that is just right for you. Don't be discouraged if your first attempts don't turn out as you expected. It will take a few "test runs" before you master the procedure. Once you begin realizing the benefits derived from makeup, you'll be hooked. Unlike destructive addictions such as drugs or alcohol, you will be hooked on something that will enhance every aspect of your life. It will become as important to you as brushing your teeth or shaving, and you may wonder how you ever got along without it.

The benefits of including makeup as part of your personal grooming regime will probably exceed any expectations set forth in this book. Men whose appearance might have been rated as average or below average can actually appear handsome, while those who are already viewed as good looking will improve the strengths of their features.

For more information about male cosmetics, contact Dorian Cosmetics, Inc., 4781 North Congress Avenue, #256, Lantana, Florida 33462, or call (800) 9-DORIAN (Toll Free).

17

The Mature Man

PERSONAL IMAGE AND SELF-ESTEEM

There is a very old invention that, even today, plays a major role in determining the level of a modern man's self-esteem. This ancient invention is the mirror. Remember how as teenagers we became upset when our faces would erupt with acne? At the time, this scourge of bad skin seemed like the worst thing that could happen to us. The mirror was telling us that we did not look good, and the result was a loss of self-esteem and self-confidence. As we reached our twenties the days of zits were over; but then, a few years later, the mirror began giving us more bad news—our hairline was receding or our waistline started to expand. Most of us grudgingly accept these visual changes, but not without varying degrees of damage to our psyche. We use clichés as defensive techniques to mask our displeasure. If we are balding we might tell people: "Grass never grows on a busy street." To justify our midriff bulge, we say things like: "It's mine and it's all paid for." When we were teenagers with bad skin, we suffered a temporary loss of confidence, but now the changes we see appear more permanent, and as our physical persona gradually ages, in our own eyes and in what we perceive to be the eyes of others, our self-confidence is jeopardized.

When the handsome young college student/athlete looks in the mirror he sees a friend showing him through clear eyes a vision that is the object of desire for many young women. He sees a face and physique free of any mark of time.

As the years pass, this friend inevitably will begin to betray him, showing lines around the eyes, a sagging chin, and puffy jowls. For this former man about campus the march of time may be even more traumatic than for the average man because the athlete has experienced, and truly knows, the favors and the privileges granted to men with handsome physical images. He slowly becomes aware that the physical treasure he took for granted is being pilfered by time, and he begins to feel increasingly angry and upset. It may be that this erosion of physical appearance is one of the reasons so many superstar athletes decline in their later years. Since most of us have never experienced the worship and adulation lavished on the handsome collegiate athlete, the prospect of aging may be somewhat less traumatic but no less painful.

The aging process is the one common life experience that all men share. In our view, it is not just loss of youth that causes men to lose self-esteem and self-confidence; it is also the loss of the visual appearance of youth. Just as we make judgments about others based on what we see, we also make judgments about ourselves based on what the mirror tells us, or what we *perceive* the mirror to be telling us. The mirror has proven itself to be a traitor and is telling us that we can no longer participate in the passion and excitement associated with youth. Over time our reflected image only serves to reinforce the negativity that continues to extinguish the flame of self-esteem and self-confidence. If you *see* yourself as old, you *will be* old.

The good news is that the mirror can be fooled. By using the components of Image Enhancement Technology, such as that offered by makeup for men, your face when you leave the house in the morning need not be the one you had when you got out of bed.

THE MATURE MAN

There is no question that the use of Image Enhancement Technology will increase among the younger segment of the male population, but what about older men? Ironically, although it is the older man who stands to benefit most from makeup and other forms of Image Enhancement Technology, he may be the most reluctant to use them. His reluctance stems from a lack of familiarity with these image-improving techniques. Human nature makes him less receptive to new ideas and changes as he ages.

The population of mature men can be divided into three main groups. Members of the first and perhaps the largest group have been married for years and are probably settled into long-term employment situations. These men perceive their lives and themselves as being very secure: they are "locked into" their personal comfort zone; "self-improvement" or "personal image" are usually forgotten terms. The second group is much smaller, consisting of mature men who thrive on challenges and new experiences in their business and personal lives. Although many pages have been taken off the calendar during their lifetime, they often possess more energy and enthusiasm than men half their age. Once the members of this group become more aware of the advantages of using makeup and other forms of Image Enhancement Technology, they will help establish a masculine standard that will be followed by future generations. The third group consists of men from the first group who for years had pictured their lives as stable but now face completely new circumstances. They may be in a position of having to start a new career, or having to meet new people and develop new relationships. Life can be extremely difficult for these men. They must realize that, during their period of inactivity, the world has changed (and continues to do so). The standards for the man of the 1990s are much different from his predecessor of the 1960s. The members of this third group can benefit most from the information we have discussed here. Earlier we talked about starting over: if you want to make a new start in life, it is necessary to put old habits and old ideas behind you. If you do not do this, you can not change anything.

1954   1994

Believe it or not, four decades have passed between these photographs of coauthor Richard Derwald, but is there a forty-year difference in his appearance? (The photograph at left was published in *Strength and Health* magazine. The photograph at right © Frank M. Luterek.)

GROW OLDER, BUT DON'T BE OLD

From the time humans accepted their mortality and the inevitability of aging, humankind has searched for that magic substance imparting eternal youth. In the sixteenth century Ponce de Leon spent years looking for the mythical Fountain of Youth. In more recent times the motion picture *Cocoon* told of magical waters made potent by visitors from outer space and how they rejuvenated sickly old people. Oscar Wilde's *Picture of Dorian Gray* tells of a man who transported his soul into a portrait; the portrait then began to age, allowing Dorian to remain young.

There is certainly nothing wrong with wanting to look young. The image of youth implies health, an alert mind, vitality, ambition, sensuality, and a passion for life. An older man who is in good shape and follows the principles outlined in this book can actually appear more virile, exuberant, and attractive than his younger counterpart, since he also has the added dimension of experience.

No doubt you have heard some older man say, "I feel exactly the same as I did twenty years ago." Often such a statement is not self-deception. He may feel younger than his years even though he does not look exactly the same as he did two decades ago. Because he looks older his life is not the same as it was when he was younger. People react to him based on his aging appearance. Many perspective employers, clients, business partners, and women see him as old. To be *older* is fine, but to *be* old is not. In society's eyes, "old" means the loss of exuberance and the lust for the rewards and passions of life. Whether social or individual in nature, perception is often more powerful than reality. A change in attitude can change the way we view ourselves and others; no matter how old we actually are, the following popular saying remains all too true: "Life is a one-time performance, this is not a dress rehearsal." Your goal should be to live every day of your life to the fullest, and the goal becomes more realistic when you feel and look your best. The information in this book can be a benefit to the older reader who still has the zest and the desire for a full and active life. We are not suggesting that you deny your age, but rather *affirm your life.*

THE IMAGE OF ATTITUDE: THE VIC BOFF STORY

In Aldous Huxley's novel *Brave New World*, people did not get physically older: they lived a full life, and when "their time came" they were sent to a special place where even their last moments were filled with happiness. It has only been in recent years that the life expectancy of the human male has caught up a bit with that of the female. One of the reasons for this discrepancy in longevity is the stress and pressure men have had to endure over the years. There are some men who have had the wisdom to "step back" and reap the benefits of a full and happy life. Richard Derwald has had the pleasure of knowing such a man. His name is Vic Boff.

One day in July of 1993, Richard spent a most interesting afternoon sitting on a patio in a condo in Cape Coral, Florida. He had responded to an invitation to have lunch with a man who many consider a living legend, Vic Boff. When Richard arrived at the condo complex Vic was standing in front of the building. Although they had never met face to face, Richard knew immediately who it was, despite the fact that most of the pictures of Vic were probably twenty-five years old. He stood there approaching his eightieth year, wearing a cut-off T-shirt that exposed muscular, suntanned arms that looked like they belonged on the body of a man many years younger. The two men strolled up to the condo, where Richard was introduced to Anne, Vic's wife of more than fifty years. They then settled on the patio overlooking a beautiful inland waterway and for the next five hours they consumed several pitchers of grapefruit juice while Richard bombarded Vic with questions. Western culture sometimes tends to dismiss the importance of the counsel and wisdom of its older citizens. During his long life, Vic had attained virtually every reward life has to offer: financial success, a good marriage, successful children, and life-long robust health. These things didn't just happen. Richard was certain that the benefit of Vic's wisdom would be priceless.

The Vic Boff story is similar to the others detailed in this book. He was an average boy who transformed his image and transformed his life.

Many middle-aged men begin having morbid thoughts about getting older. The fact is that our entire stay on this planet can be a glorious and stimulating experience if we take advantage of one simple truth: happiness based on self-confidence is the key to a long and fulfilling life.

After more than sixty years of study and experience in "the art of living," Vic lives by a basic philosophy. His secret involves what he calls the "pleasure or pain pendulum." In our lifetime we will all experience periods of both pleasure and pain. Vic sees these things as being at opposite ends of a swinging pendulum: pleasure on one side, pain on the other. The secret to maintaining good health and success is keeping that pendulum on the pleasure side.

"The basis of pleasure is found in health; the realization of pleasure is found through success. By success I do not necessarily mean money; success means accomplishment and self-satisfaction. When some men experience a radical change in their lives—such as retirement, the loss of a job, the loss of a spouse, or a divorce—they start to feel worthless. This feeling is unwarranted because real and lasting self-worth comes from within ourselves. When we have this feeling of useful self-worth and self-confidence, it will positively effect not only our life but the lives of those around us."

Vic Boff's entire life has been a manifestation of self-confidence, of mind over matter. He has become world famous as a charter member of the Iceberg Athletic Club. This club is comprised of a group of hearty men who swim in the frigid waters of the Atlantic Ocean during the coldest winter months. In 1967, Vic spent a record forty-two minutes swimming in water that registered only forty degrees. His length of time in that cold water exceeded the existing record by twenty-two minutes. On Sunday December 28th, Vic spent a record twelve hours on the beach at Coney Island and went into the frigid water every hour on the hour. While he was splashing around in the ocean, New York City was suffering through the coldest weather of the season at seven degrees below zero.

Vic says that by conditioning his body to the attitude of cold, he conditioned his mind to the attitude of success. For the past few years Vic has been enjoying

After more than sixty years, Vic Boff is still enthusiastic about life, full of energy, and in great physical shape!

the climate of the sunny South, but says he still misses those invigorating winter dips.

Conquering the challenge of frigid cold helped develop a blueprint for Vic Boff's life. He is so positive about life that he will not allow any negative remarks during a conversation. He believes negativity breeds depression. He knows we all will encounter some hard times, but our lives are like a ship: when it rocks we have to straighten it out.

Vic Boff still works out and swims every day. He is in great demand as a consultant to the fitness industry, and is constantly asked to appear at various health and fitness expos around the world.

Though we wouldn't dare to suggest that anyone reading this book should go swimming in freezing water, nonetheless, we all have our own challenges, and the way we handle these challenges will determine whether our pendulum will be swinging toward pleasure or pain.

Vic Boff serves as a shining example for all who think their best days are behind them. Thanks to a positive attitude and Image Enhancement Technology, he is alive with enthusiasm and makes plans for each new tomorrow. Vic Boff's classic book *You Can Be Physically Perfect, Powerfully Strong* is now in its tenth printing and he is currently working on a new book to be released soon.

Though the phrase is now a cliché, "Tomorrow is the first day of the rest of your life." Any man, whether eighteen or eighty, can start over. Colonel Sanders of Kentucky Fried Chicken fame became a millionaire after his sixtieth birthday. Former surgeon general C. Everett Koop is quoted as saying, "Age sixty-five is not old anymore, a man of eighty-seven today is at the same point in his life expectancy as a sixty-five-year-old man was at the turn of the century."

When Satchel Paige, the great star of the old Negro baseball league, was asked his age by a newspaper reporter, Satchel responded by saying, "How old would you be if you didn't know how old you were?"

SUMMARY

Image Enhancement Technology is a "key to success" for the man of today. The effects of this science will:

- MAKE YOU HEALTHIER

- MAKE YOU MORE MUSCULAR

- MAKE YOU TALLER

- MAKE YOU THINNER

- MAKE YOU BETTER LOOKING

and these things will:

- HELP MAKE YOU SELF-CONFIDENT

- HELP MAKE YOU HAPPY

- HELP MAKE YOU SUCCESSFUL

You may still be unsure that Image Enhancement Technology can help you. We understand how you feel. There are so many hollow promises in the world today; it is only natural for you to be skeptical. But more than you realize or may care to admit, the way you look has a tremendous impact on the direction of your life. The way you look is a significant factor in how you feel about yourself. You deserve to feel your very best! Modern technology has found ways to compensate for and control elements of physical appearance that for years remained sources of frustration and discouragement for many a man. You now have the means to transform your image and transform your life.

IT'S YOUR LIFE . . .

IT'S YOUR IMAGE . . .

IT'S YOUR CHOICE . . .

Coauthors Richard Derwald, age sixty; and Anthony Chiappone, age thirty-one (Photograph © Frank M. Luterek)

About the Authors

Richard J. Derwald and Anthony C. Chiappone founded the first and at present the only company marketing makeup for men. Due to their personal life experiences, both of these men are uniquely qualified in the area of masculine image enhancement. The nearly three decades that separates them (Richard is sixty and Anthony thirty one) permit them to understand and speak to men of all age groups. Both Richard and Anthony have the background to address the total spectrum of image transformation since they have personally been the beneficiaries of much of the technology detailed in these pages.

Many books are written by authors who have researched a certain subject, but this volume is based on contemporary realities and firsthand knowledge. The transformation of your total image, head to toe, is now made possible by the various enhancement technologies detailed in these pages. The authors are products of this technology. The following personal profiles show how each of them has utilized the benefits of this technology. These brief biographies should illustrate that although you may not have been born muscular or handsome, it is now possible for you to achieve the image you always wanted.

THE DORIAN STORY: RICHARD J. DERWALD

As a young boy growing up in the 1940s, many of my heroes were those I watched every Saturday afternoon at the movie theater. There was Buster Crabbe as Flash Gordon, and Johnny Weissmuller as Tarzan. I admired those fearless strongmen of the silver screen, and I always imagined myself playing those parts. Unfortunately, the reality of my life at that time was very different. I was far below average in athletic ability and was always the last one to be chosen when picking sides for any team sport. One day I purchased an issue of the magazine *Physical Culture* published by Bernarr Macfadden. I read and reread the stories showing before and after photos of people who transformed their bodies through exercise and diet. If the information in *Physical Culture* was true, then I could transform my own image, which I felt would help change my life.

The year was 1950, and at that time there were no commercial gyms in the Buffalo area, and neither sporting goods stores nor department stores sold weights. I had to get my first barbell set through mail order. In the 1990s, with millions of people buying memberships in the giant health club chains such as Gold's and Balley's, it's difficult to imagine that only a few decades ago this type of physical activity was frowned upon.

During the first year of weight training I gained about forty pounds. My physical appearance was so improved that even some of my own relatives didn't recognize me. Many of my former grammar school classmates who had given me a hard time in the past now wanted to be my friends. Inspired by my bodybuilding success, a friend named Bob Fitzgerald began training with me. As in many big city neighborhoods we had a local hero—his name was Don Lewin. Don was becoming very successful working as a professional wrestler. Being young and confident, Bob and I agreed that we could be wrestlers, too. After a short training period, we entered a small-time wrestling circuit and had immediate success winning the Western New York State Tag Team Championship belts. We were very optimistic and our plan was to go to New York City and get booked into Madison Square

Garden. We figured we were on our way when Bob got called up in the draft, so I decided to continue wrestling solo.

Even though I was making good money, my parents were against my choice of professions. I explained to them many times that it was only a show and nobody got hurt. The second part of my story was not exactly true: I did get a little banged up. One night I wrestled some jerk who must not have known it was only a show. We wound up slugging away at each other. After the match I knew I was in trouble. I had found myself nursing a swollen eye and nose along with some assorted scratches and bruises. If I were to show up at home in such a condition, my parents would have hit the ceiling.

While driving home from the arena with my girlfriend, I expressed concern about my scars of battle. She looked at my face and said, "I think I have something that will help." She reached in her purse and took out a plastic case. "This will hide the bumps and bruises," she said. The round, flat case contained pancake makeup. (It got its name from the shape of its container rather than the contents.) When she applied the makeup to my face, she insisted that it be evenly distributed. After she finished I was amazed when I looked in the rear-view mirror: the bumps, bruises, and swelling could hardly be seen. But even more significant was that I appeared better-looking. Five years earlier a copy of *Physical Culture* magazine placed me on the road to transforming my body; now in only a few minutes I learned that I could also transform my facial appearance.

Eventually I decided to quit wrestling and change my life in a more positive direction. Since my education ended with high school, I enrolled in college to pursue a degree in accounting. But I was pretty low on cash. My experience as a professional wrestler gave me a flair for show business, so I figured I could make some money as an entertainer in the new music craze called rock 'n' roll. Because my bodyweight of two hundred and twenty pounds was much too heavy for an entertainer, it was time for another image transformation. I embarked on a program consisting of a weight-reduction diet and aerobics to bring my weight down to one hundred seventy-six pounds. In order to attain the rock 'n' roll image, I let my hair grow and added a great set of Elvis-style sideburns. Many people who had not seen me for a while did not recognize me. I also noticed that my interactions with people altered as my image changed; they weren't really better or worse, just different.

I had become a self-taught expert on the subject of makeup and with some effort I was able to find a few products that looked natural. This was important since my schedule of five days in school and three or four nights a week in night-clubs left me looking a bit haggard. But thanks to makeup my fatigue seldom showed through.

When I began my job hunt I knew that there was no place in the corporate world for my long hair and sideburns, so it was time for another change of image. It was during the job interview process that I began to wear a shirt and tie every day. I finally obtained a position in the accounting department of the Hydronics Division of American Standard, Inc.

In several years I was able to progress from the position of accountant to Director of Data Processing, a position I held for more than ten years. During that time I married my wife, Maureen, and started a family (a son, Richie, and a daughter, Kathy). Things were really going well, then the roof fell in. A corporate decision was made to close the plant.

I had been very comfortable but now I was in a panic. I had a young family and had worked my way up to a position that now called for a master's degree. I was forty years old and had not had a job interview in twenty years. I had become too comfortable and soft, sliding into the relaxed state of middle age. My increasing waistline was matched only by my receding hairline. I had become an out-of-shape, balding, middle-aged corporate manager who was about to lose his world. The time had come when I had to make a strong impression if I had any chance of continuing to earn a living. The notice of the plant closing gave me about five months to prepare for the job market. Although I did not have an advanced degree I could count on a very strong resume and references. Unfortunately I knew it might take more than that to land a worthwhile management position. After years in my comfort zone, it was time to start over, and I began again to transform my image.

Going back to the workouts and the diet, I could lose the weight but I couldn't reverse my receding hairline. I hated to look at any photographs of myself since I looked even more bald than I imagined. But baldness was far more preferable, in my view, than some ridiculous toupee. Because there were no other options, I went hair shopping.

I was delighted to find a hair replacement that looked natural. One of the most vivid recollections of my life was the first time I saw myself wearing the replacement. It almost seemed as though it was another person looking back at me in the mirror. Over the years I had forgotten how I looked with a full head of hair. Why had I spent so many years resigned to going bald? It was during this period that I made a promise to myself: in the future I would never again allow my image to deteriorate. I had finally learned that, through no fault of my own, adversity can suddenly happen in my life and I must always be at my personal best to turn things around.

In March 1975, I went for my first interview in more than two decades. I had responded to an ad for director of management information services at the Transportation Equipment Division of Dresser Industries. When I left the house the day of the interview, I was ready.

During the course of the interview, the personnel director told me that he thought he may have brought in the wrong candidate because I didn't look forty. With more than fifty applicants to choose from, and after two more interviews, I got the job. In retrospect, losing my previous job was the best thing that ever happened. There used to be a television commercial for a men's aftershave in which a guy would get slapped and say "Thanks, I needed that." Losing my job was the slap in the face that I needed. Though I had a great deal of success at Dresser, and I enjoyed my work, I was never quite the same again. In the back of my mind my thoughts were focused on controlling my own destiny and starting my own business.

In 1983, Dresser announced the closing of the transportation equipment division. Unlike my previous experience, this time I was prepared. I was offered a position in Dresser's Heidelberg, Germany, division. The position would have meant much more money and the opportunity for gaining status in an international corporation. The decision to start my own business would have been much easier had they not offered me the job. After much thought, I stuck to my guns and cut the corporate cord.

That same year I opened "Head to Toe," a total-image salon. Developing the business was very stimulating; it seemed to enhance my creative thought processes. Then, in 1984, I developed the idea to make toy action figures of World Wrestling Federation (WWF) stars. I sold this idea to the LJN toy company in New York and was gratified to learn that it produced one of the largest-selling items in the history of the toy industry.

The story of Dorian Cosmetics began one evening in 1985. My daughter, Kathy, had a date with a young man to attend a dinner dance for his company. When he arrived at our home he looked terrible. He was just getting over an attack of the flu and it had taken its toll on his appearance. He mentioned that because he looked so bad, maybe they should skip the dinner and go somewhere else. Kathy knew that I had mastered the art of makeup for men, so she asked if I could do something. Her date was very reluctant to allow me to put makeup on his face, but Kathy insisted. After I was done and he looked in the mirror, he had the same look that I had when I first used makeup. He was astounded. Kathy later told me that during the evening he stopped at every mirror. Soon thereafter Kathy turned to me and asked, "Dad, why don't you start a company and sell these cosmetics for men?"

Thanks to Image Enhancement Technology I looked good for a guy over fifty. Some people would kid me, asking if I had a picture of myself in the attic that was getting older instead of me. Based on my daughter's suggestion, I formed Dorian Cosmetics, the first company to market makeup for men.

ANTHONY C. CHIAPPONE

Earlier we discussed the fact that all men are not created equal. I believe that most people who achieve any degree of success in their lives had to overcome obstacles to reach their goal. I am convinced that most of the major personalities in the sport of bodybuilding started out by overcoming feelings of personal inadequacy. This should not be viewed as a negative statement; the flame of achievement is fanned by desire. The pages of this book contain stories about average men who desired and attained a superior image. I believe that, like Richard Derwald, I am qualified to give testimony to the reality of image transformation and the secrets of a successful image.

At the age of one I experienced a severe physical trauma. Although I was too young to remember the details, my parents explained the incident. While I was seated in my high chair the baby sitter who was watching me left the room. During that short period, I managed to tip the high chair, falling backwards onto the concrete floor. The baby sitter carefully picked me up and placed me in the crib and immediately called my parents and an ambulance. When I arrived at the hospital emergency room I had only a faint heartbeat and was diagnosed as suffering from a subdermal hematoma: an overabundance of blood was rushing to an area of my brain because of the major fracture to the skull I had received as a result of the fall. The surgeon had no choice but to operate. He made a five-inch incision along the left side of my head to relieve the pressure. I lapsed into a coma as my terrified parents stood vigil for several days.

After being released from the hospital, I carried some momentos of this incident, which included a five-inch scar along the left side of my head. The operation also altered some of my facial features: for example, my left eye was noticeably larger than my right eye.

During my grammar school years I dreamed about excelling in athletics. My parents' only concern was that my health would continue to improve. As I reached adolescence and entered high school, I became acutely aware of my physical appearance and developed a burning desire to improve. My grandfather, who had come to the United States from Sicily along with my father, had started a road construction business many years before and by the time I was in my teens this business had grown into a very successful family operation. My older brother, Chris, was already working in our road-paving business, and I wanted to make my contribution.

My first summer on the job was really tough because the medication prescribed during my childhood had taken a toll on my physical strength. Shoveling blacktop in the hot summer sun was not an easy task. At the end of that first summer I returned to high school and joined a gym. Although I may have lost some of the physical abilities, my desire to improve was reflected in a rigorous four-day-a-week exercise schedule. Over time, I gradually improved, and in my junior year of high school I earned a starting position on both the hockey and lacrosse teams.

The scar on the side of my head served as a constant reminder of how fortunate I was to be alive and healthy. Considering the seriousness of the fall, the outcome could have been much worse.

My appreciation of life and the value of living it to the fullest was never more intense than during the period when I watched my mother fight a four-year battle with cancer. Diagnosed with breast cancer during my freshman year of college, her malignancy continued to spread, destroying her little by little. On my birthday four years later, she died. More than ever, I realized how important it was to make the most of life. Exercise, diet, and striving to be the best I could were, for me, elements of a full, rich life. Shortly after my mother's death a college friend passed on to me a philosophy of life that has remained with me to this day: "We have a long way to go and a short time to get there."

During my college years I had occasion to meet the director of a local modeling agency and was more than a little surprised when I was asked to model some men's clothing at an upcoming fashion show. Apparently the agency was pleased with my work; during my final year of college I was able to earn extra money working as a model.

I believe that if each of us looks back in time we can recall at least one incident that seemed insignificant but which actually helped define the course of our lives. One evening while working out at the gym, I mentioned that I was upset because I had a modeling job the next day and my face had broken out. This particular job was very important because it was the biggest show of the year. The person I was talking to happened to be Richard Derwald, a regular at the gym. After his workout, Richard went down to the locker room and came back with a small black leather case. He explained that the case contained a unique collection of men's cosmetics, which would help cover my skin problem for the show. Needless to say, I was apprehensive. Having been raised in a family of construction workers, the idea of men wearing makeup was hard to fathom.

The contents of that small black leather case not only covered up the problem, it also made my appearance the most successful of the afternoon. As a result, I was immediately offered a spot on a television commercial for a local bedding company. After the show I was besieged with inquiries from everyone about how I had enhanced my appearance. The pent-up demand for the benefits of men's makeup became very apparent.

I had just graduated from college with a degree in business and had committed to go to Boston to take a marketing position. My main interest was with the family construction business, but I wanted to work a few years in some other environment to gain additional experience. I was sorry I had made this commitment because I knew that I really wanted to be in the men's cosmetics business. Prior to my departure for Boston I arranged a partnership agreement with Richard and became vice president of Dorian Cosmetics, Inc.

When I returned from Boston we launched an international campaign featuring three quarter-page advertisements in major bodybuilding publications. Through these efforts Dorian Cosmetics has experienced a 400-percent increase in volume over the past three years. Our customer base extends well beyond the United States to Canada, the United Kingdom, Europe, Africa, Australia, and parts of Asia. We currently have thousands of customers who reorder on a regular basis.

There are three things in your life that are important and each one will be inscribed on your tombstone: the date you were born, the date you died, and the dash between these dates. The dash is the most important thing.

Bibliography

Danoff, Dudley Seth, M.D., and David S. Katz, PA-C. "Erection Resurrection," *Muscle and Fitness* (June 1994).

Galwip, Houston Mary. *A Technical History of Costumes*. London, England: A. C. Black, 1954.

Geoffrrey, Squire. *Dress and Society 1560–1970*. New York: Viking Press, 1974.

Godfrey, Lionel. *Cary Grant*. New York: St. Martin's, 1981.

Griffin, Cary. "The Penis: Its Size and Function," *Muscular Development* (March 1994).

Hartt, Frederick. *Art: A History of Painting, Sculpture, and Architecture*. New York: Harry L. Abrams, 1976.

Macfadden, Mary, and Emile Gauvreau. *Dumbbells and Carrot Strips*. New York: Henry Holt and Company, 1953.

Maron, Michael. *Instant Makeover Magic*. New York: Warner Books, 1983.

Schwarzenegger, Arnold, and Douglas K. Hall. *Arnold: The Education of a Bodybuilder*. New York: Pocket Books, 1982.

Woodforde, John. *The History of Vanity*. New York: St. Martin's, 1992.

Appendix

The following brief list of publications may help you in developing the style and flair that is uniquely you.

Details
P.O. Box 58246
Boulder, CO 80322
(800) 627-6367 (Toll Free)

Esquire
Hearst Corporation
250 W. 55th Street
New York, NY 10019
(800) 888-5400 (Toll Free)

Exercise For Men Only
Chelo Publishing, Inc.
350 Fifth Avenue
New York, NY 10118
(212) 947-4322

GQ (*Gentleman's Quarterly*)
Conde Nast Publishing, Inc.
350 Madison Avenue
New York, NY 10017
(800) 289-9330 (Toll Free)

International Male (catalog)
741 F Street
P.O. Box 129027
San Diego, CA 92112-9027
(800) 293-9333 (Toll Free)

Men's Exercise
Pumpkin Press, Inc.
350 Fifth Avenue, Suite 8216
New York, NY 10018
(212) 947-4322

Men's Health
Rodale Press, Inc.
33 E. Minor Street
Emmaus, PA 18098
(215) 967-5171

Natural Bodybuilding and Fitness
Chelo Publishing, Inc.
350 Fifth Avenue
New York, NY 10118
(212) 947-4322

Playboy
P.O. Box 5209
Harlan, IA 51593-2709
(800) 652-1200 (Toll Free)

OF